Kira and Henry

Dangerous Treaty

A Young Adult Fantasy

By
Sandi Jerome

Kira and Henry

Dangerous Treaty

A Young Adult Fantasy

By
Sandi Jerome

SmilingEagle Press Book

1st Edition

© 2025 by Sandi Jerome

Published by SmilingEagle Press
www.smilingeagle.com

Print ISBN: 978-1-969767-99-9
e-book ISBN: 978-1-969767-04-3
Printed in the United States of America

Cover Design by: Nilesh Prabhu
author.nileshprabhu@gmail.com

Map and drawings by: Tulaasi Jerome
https://www.etsy.com/shop/RainbowJunkieINC

Dedication

This book is dedicated to my fearless women warriors; Chandra, Suby, Tulaasi and Vrinda who have made my life an adventure and my husband Keith who has taken the ride with me.

Kira and Henry

Dangerous Treaty
A Young Adult Fantasy

Map of the Kingdom

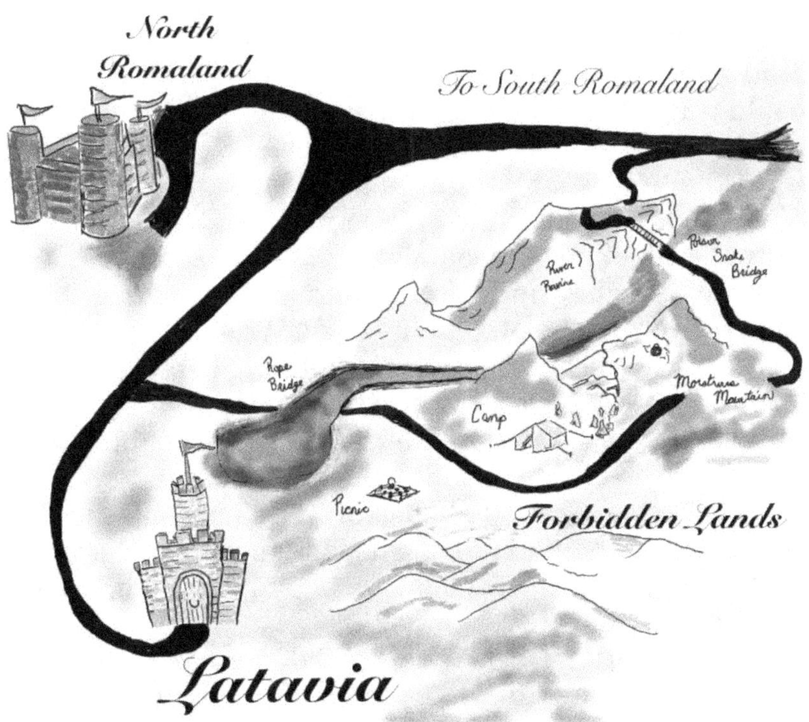

Prologue

Princess Kira stared at the trolls roasted on silver platters and wondered how she'd reached this moment. She was in a hostile castle, being ordered to eat creatures who had trusted her, facing a choice between compromising her soul and starting a war.

How did I get here?

She could trace it back through the mistakes and victories that had brought her to this feast of horror. Each choice had seemed necessary at the time, each compromise smaller than the next. But they'd led her here, to Prince William's great hall, where the cost of principles had never been higher.

At least, she thought grimly, *it could have been worse.*

She had faced worse before, hadn't she? Though sitting here now, watching nobles expect her to eat thinking beings, it was hard to remember any situation quite this impossible.

Her mind drifted back to that moment in the enchanted forest, hanging upside down from ancient trees with faces. Francis, Ida, and Mabel, the tree sisters who had captured her and Henry. She had been completely helpless then, suspended by magical vines hundreds of feet in the air, at the mercy of beings who had every reason to hate humans.

"Where are our children?" Francis had demanded, her bark-face twisted with grief and fury. *"Tell us what you humans did with our saplings!"*

Kira had thought she was going to die then. She thought the trees would crush her for crimes she had not committed, for sins of other humans who'd harvested their young without understanding. She had talked her way through it, convinced them she was not their enemy, and earned their trust enough to escape with her life.

She had thought *that* was the worst situation she had ever faced. How naive she had been.

And before that, the poisoned snake bridge almost killed her. Kira's raptor blood stirred at the memory, her hidden wings pressing against the bindings beneath her gown. She had watched her horse tumble down the ravine. Henry had scolded her for not knowing her horse's name. At one point, she feared that Henry thought she was a monster.

But tonight, Prince William **was** the monster. He was the one who smiled while planning cruelty. He dressed barbarity in diplomatic language and expected her to call it civilization. He had trapped her not with vines or venom, but with impossible choices where every option led to suffering.

Her thoughts jumped further back, to a different kind of impossible situation. The twin trolls, Peek and Aboo, seemed impossible to conquer when she had first encountered them in the forbidden lands. They had planned to eat Kira and Henry, but Kira had stood strong with her sword and her conviction that eating thinking beings was wrong, especially when she was the one who could be eaten.

She had been right then. It had been clear and simple. Trolls should not eat humans because humans could think and feel and didn't deserve to be food.

So why was Prince William now forcing her to do exactly what she had condemned? Why was the line between civilization and monstrosity suddenly so blurred that she could barely see it?

Because Romaland makes everything complicated, she realized. *They take simple moral questions and wrap them in politics and threats until you cannot remember what was right anymore.*

But she *could* remember. She closed her eyes briefly, ignoring the expectant nobles watching her, ignoring Prince William's predatory smile. She remembered her mother, Queen Kirena with her hidden wings, her secret heritage, her thousand daily compromises to protect her family.

"A wise ruler doesn't need the sword," her mother had said. *"But sometimes, the sword is what justice demands."*

Kira had thought she understood that lesson. She had thought her mother meant knowing when to fight and when to negotiate.

But now, sitting at this table with Prince William's ultimatum hanging in the air, she finally understood the deeper truth.

Her mother had hidden her own wings her entire life, making compromise after compromise, swallowing her pride, pretending to be something she was not, all to protect what mattered. But there had been one thing she never compromised on: her daughter. Her mother's fundamental values centered on what made life worth living. But Kira had killed her mother. Yes, nobody blamed her for her mother's death, nobody except herself.

And when the plague came to the castle gates, when Queen Kirena could have saved herself by fleeing, she stayed. She had chosen principle over survival, had died rather than abandon the sick children who needed her care.

That is what her mother's lesson meant. Not that you should never compromise, but that you had to know where your final line was. Survival sometimes meant surrender.

Kira had been looking for that line since she arrived in Romaland. She had crossed so many smaller ones, like nearly eating a sprite in that flower sprite cake, or the young trolls while smiling diplomatically. Each time she had told herself it was a strategy, that she was buying time, gathering intelligence, serving a greater good.

But with each compromise, she had lost a piece of herself. And Prince William knew it. He had *planned* it. He had been breaking her down systematically, testing how far she'd bend before she broke.

Well, Kira thought, opening her eyes and meeting Prince William's gaze with renewed clarity, *he's about to find out.*

She thought about Henry beside her, loyal despite everything. About Freddy, the brave little frog who had come with them to Romaland, knowing he might become someone's dinner. About Elena and her resistance network, people who'd been fighting this fight for years with no guarantee of victory. About Peek and Aboo, captured trying to rescue her because friendship mattered more than safety.

They had all drawn their lines. They had all chosen what they stood for, even when standing meant falling.

It is my turn, Kira realized. *This is my moment. My mother's moment was the plague. Henry's moment was choosing to stay with me instead of finding his birth family. This is mine.*

She looked at the roasted trolls on their silver platters. Looked at Prince William's expectant expression. Looked at the Romalander nobles waiting to see if Latavian values were real or just pretty words that crumbled under pressure.

And she knew, with absolute certainty. Whatever came next, whatever it cost, she couldn't eat what was on those platters. She could not pretend that this was acceptable. She couldn't compromise one more time. If she did —if she bent this one last time, there would be no coming back. She would have proven Prince William right: that everyone had a breaking point, that Latavian compassion was just weakness waiting to be exploited, that in the end, survival mattered more than principles.

At least it could have been worse, she thought one final time, taking a strange comfort in the idea. She had survived enchanted forests and poison snake bridge, twin trolls and political intrigue. She had faced death before and would face it again.

But she had never faced it with such clarity about who she was and what she stood for.

Princess Kira straightened her spine, lifted her chin, and prepared to say the word that would change everything: *No!*

Whatever happened next, at least she'd meet it as herself. Not as a broken diplomat or a compromised princess or someone who had learned to call evil by pretty names.

Kira, Princess of Latavia, loving daughter of a queen who'd known where to draw the line.

This moment was when she drew hers.

Chapter 1 - The Romalander Delegation

The morning sun painted Castle Latavia's stone towers in shades of amber and gold, but Princess Kira felt no warmth as she stood beside Sir Henry on the eastern battlements. Her hand rested on her sword hilt, fingers drumming an anxious rhythm against the leather-wrapped handle. Below them, the main courtyard bustled with preparations for the arrival of Prince William's delegation.

"They're late," Kira observed, her raptor-sharp eyes scanning the distant tree line where the forest road emerged from shadow. "Romalanders pride themselves on punctuality. It's a power play."

Henry shifted beside her, his own gaze tracking the movements of servants arranging tables in the courtyard. "Or perhaps they're simply ensuring their provisions arrive intact. It's a long journey from Romaland."

"You're too generous with them," Kira said, though her tone held more concern than criticism. "These are the people who allowed you to be captured, knowing you'd be enslaved, Henry. How can you speak so calmly about their arrival?"

Henry's jaw tightened almost imperceptibly. Yes, Romaland didn't fight for him, but it was Latavia who enslaved him until the king made him his ward and a playmate for the princess.

"Because someone must, Princess. If we approach this with only anger, we'll have war before the feast is even served."

Kira turned to study her friend's profile. The frightened boy who had clutched a wooden horse toy so hard it left marks on his palm had grown into a knight whose scars, both visible and hidden, ran deeper than most knew. She reached over and squeezed his arm briefly. "You're right. I know you're right. It doesn't mean I have to like it."

A trumpet blast echoed across the valley, sharp and clear in the morning air. Both straightened as a line of riders emerged from the forest, their purple and silver banners snapping in the breeze. At the head of the column rode a figure whose bearing screamed nobility even from this distance.

"There," Henry said quietly. "Prince William's ambassadors."

As the delegation drew closer, Kira could make out more details. The lead rider wore armor that gleamed like liquid silver, far finer than anything in Castle Latavia's armory. Behind him came a wagon train – no, three wagon trains – covered in heavy canvas and surrounded by armed guards.

"That's a lot of provisions for a diplomatic visit," Kira muttered.

"The Romalanders never travel light," Henry replied, but she heard the uncertainty threading through his words. He'd noticed it too: the unusual size of the escort, the way the guards' hands never strayed far from their weapons.

King Phillip emerged from the keep below, resplendent in his formal robes. Queen Selina stood at his side, her composure perfect despite the early hour. Kira thought about how much the queen had changed from a wicked stepmother into a comfort to her father.

Kira watched him take his position at the base of the grand staircase, every inch the gracious host, and felt a surge of admiration. He'd been against this meeting from the start, but now that circumstances demanded it, he would perform his role flawlessly.

"We should join them," Henry said, already moving toward the stairs.

Kira followed, her boots ringing on the stone steps as they descended. By the time they reached the courtyard, the lead riders had entered through the main gate. Up close, the Romalander delegation was even more impressive and intimidating. Their armor bore no marks of travel, as if they'd somehow journeyed through the wilderness without collecting a single speck of dust.

The lead ambassador, Lord Marcus, dismounted with fluid grace and swept into a bow that managed to be both perfectly correct and somehow condescending. "Your Majesty," he said, his voice carrying across the courtyard. "May I present, Prince William of Romaland."

One of the knights came forward, lifted his helmet and nodded.

"Prince William!" King Phillip replied, inclining his head. "You and your party are most welcome. Castle Latavia stands ready to host you with all the hospitality our realm can provide."

Prince Willaims's eyes swept across the assembled Latavians, lingering on Kira and Henry before moving on. Something in that gaze made Kira's skin prickle – it was the way a hunter might assess prey before deciding whether it was worth the chase.

"We are honored by your generosity," Lord Marcus said smoothly. "Prince William has brought gifts appropriate to such an auspicious occasion. If Your Majesty permits, we would be pleased to unload them immediately."

King Phillip gestured his assent, and the wagons began rolling forward. Servants rushed to assist with unloading, but the Romalander guards barked orders in their harsh dialect, insisting on handling the cargo themselves. The first crates that emerged contained what appeared to be luxury goods; fine fabrics, jeweled goblets, and intricately carved furniture.

But it was the last wagon that drew everyone's attention. As the canvas was pulled back, a strange smell wafted across the courtyard. It was not quite rotten, but preserved, pungent, making several servants step back involuntarily.

"What is that?" Kira whispered to Henry.

"Romalander provisions," he replied, his face carefully neutral. "They always bring their own food to foreign courts."

"But what kind of food smells like that?"

"You don't want to know, trust me in this."

Lord Marcus had noticed their exchange. He smiled, and something about that expression reminded Kira of a snake coiling before a strike. "Ah, I see curiosity about our traditional delicacies. Rest assured, we would never impose our particular tastes on our gracious hosts. These provisions are purely for our own consumption."

The afternoon passed in a blur of formal greetings and ceremonial exchanges. Kira stood through it all, maintaining the pleasant mask she'd been trained to wear on such occasions while her mind raced. Something was wrong here. She couldn't put her finger on what exactly, but every instinct honed through years of training screamed warnings. *Why had they sent word that Prince William would not attend, but he came disguised as a knight?*

As the sun began its descent toward the western horizon, nobody had seen the prince until servants announced that the welcoming feast was prepared. The great hall had been transformed, its usual stark functionality softened by tapestries and garlands of late-summer flowers. The massive oak tables gleamed with polish, set with Castle Latavia's finest dinnerware.

Kira entered with Henry at her side; both now dressed in formal attire. She'd chosen a deep red gown that accommodated her hidden wings while still allowing freedom of movement, her mother's old trick. Henry wore the red-and-gold accents of a Latavian knight, his hand resting casually near his sword hilt, a gesture that had become second nature.

The seating arrangement had been carefully planned. King Phillip and Queen Selina occupied the high table's center, with Prince William and Lord Marcus to their right. To their left sat Kira and Henry, and beside them...

Kira's breath caught as two massive figures entered the hall, stooping low to fit through the doorway.

"Peek! Aboo!" she exclaimed, unable to suppress her delight. The twin trolls – still joined by their shared tunic and still identical in their endearing ugliness – grinned at her with genuine affection.

"Princess!" Peek boomed, his voice rattling the windows. "We were invited to a fancy dinner!"

"King Phillip said we are heroes," Aboo added proudly. "Must sit at the royal table."

Kira laughed, the sound bright and genuine in the formal atmosphere. "Of course you're heroes. You helped save the enchanted forest on your first quest. You've earned a place of honor."

As the trolls settled into their reinforced chairs – specially constructed after King Phillip had learned of their invitation – Kira glanced across the table. Prince William and Lord Marcus had gone absolutely rigid, their faces cycling through expressions of shock, disgust, and barely controlled outrage.

"Your Majesty," Lord Marcus said, his cultured voice tight with strain. "Surely there has been some mistake. These... creatures... they cannot possibly be seated at the royal table with my prince."

"There's no mistake," King Phillip replied calmly. "Peek and Aboo are honored guests of the crown. They fought alongside Sir Henry to protect our realm."

"But they're trolls!" Lord Marcus's voice rose slightly before he caught himself. "In Romaland, such beings are – well, they're certainly not dinner companions."

"In Latavia," Queen Selina interjected with gentle firmness, "we judge beings by their actions, not their appearance. Peek and Aboo have proven themselves loyal friends to the kingdom." Kira smiled at this. Like Henry, Queen Selina was a Romalander by birth. She became a Latavian by marriage, and Henry... well, that was another story. She glanced fondly at him. He looked magnificent. Prince William threw down his napkin and left the room.

Lord Marcus opened his mouth to call to him, then seemed to think better of it. He settled back in his chair, but the look he directed at the trolls promised nothing good. The other Romalander delegates whispered among themselves, their expressions ranging from scandalized to openly hostile.

Servers began bringing out the feast, and Kira felt a small swell of pride at what Castle Latavia's kitchens had produced. The tables groaned under platters of roasted vegetables glistening with herb butter, steaming bowls of grain dishes studded with nuts and dried fruits, whole roasted turkeys with crispy golden skin, and several magnificent salmon presented on beds of watercress. Baskets of fresh bread – still warm from the ovens – sat at intervals along the tables, alongside wheels of cheese and crocks of butter.

It was a feast fit for royalty, carefully planned to showcase Latavian hospitality and abundance. But as the Romalander delegates began examining the offerings, their expressions grew increasingly dismayed.

"Where's the meat?" one of them muttered, loudly enough to be overheard.

"There's turkey," his companion replied. "And fish."

"Birds and fish," the first man scoffed. "I mean real meat. Venison, boar, beef. Something substantial. Beasts to be hunted and conquered."

Lord Marcus sampled a spoonful of the grain dish, his face contorting as if he'd bitten into something sour. "This is... grain? With vegetables?" He set down his spoon with exaggerated care. "In Romaland, such fare is what we feed to livestock, not honored guests."

Kira felt Henry tense beside her. She placed a warning hand on his arm, then smiled sweetly at Lord Marcus. "The feast was prepared according to Latavian tradition. We find that lighter cuisine allows for clearer thinking and sharper reflexes – both valuable qualities for knights and diplomats alike."

"Light, indeed," Lord Marcus replied. "One might even say insubstantial. In Romaland, we believe strength comes from... heartier provisions. The meat of the land, one might say." His gaze flickered to the trolls and away, too quickly to be coincidence.

An uncomfortable silence descended over the high table. King Phillip broke it with practiced diplomacy, launching into a formal toast that the Romalanders were obliged to acknowledge. But the tension remained... thick as smoke.

As the feast continued, Kira noticed the Romalander delegates eating sparingly, pushing food around their plates more than consuming it. Meanwhile, their servants had begun bringing in covered dishes from those mysterious wagons – provisions meant for the delegation's private consumption.

One of these dishes passed close enough to Kira that she caught a whiff of its contents. The smell was distinctive – preserved meat, yes, but something else underneath. Something that made her stomach turn, even as her mind struggled to identify it.

Peek leaned over to examine one of the covered dishes, his enormous nose twitching. "Smells funny," he announced to the table at large. "Like... like talking horses."

The statement hung in the air. Lord Marcus went very still.

"Talking horses?" Queen Selina repeated carefully.

"In the enchanted forest, some wild horses talk," Aboo explained helpfully. "They tell jokes, very funny, and this smells like them, except... dead."

Lord Marcus recovered his composure with visible effort. "Your trolls have remarkable imaginations. I assure you, the provisions are simple preserved meats – nothing more exotic than what any traveling party might carry."

But Kira had seen the flash of something in his eyes before he'd shuttered his expression. Not guilt, exactly. More like... satisfaction? As if he'd wanted them to know, to be disturbed by the implications.

Henry pushed his own plate away, his appetite clearly gone. Kira couldn't blame him. If Peek's nose was right – and trolls had excellent senses – then the Romalanders had brought something far more troubling than standard travel rations.

The feast dragged on, toast following toast in the tedious ritual of diplomacy. Lord Marcus made a speech praising the "quaint customs" of Latavia. King Phillip responded with carefully worded hopes for mutual understanding. Through it all, Kira watched the Romalander delegates, noting how they clustered together, how their eyes constantly assessed their surroundings, how they treated even friendly servants with contempt.

These weren't diplomats seeking peace. They were scouts, gathering intelligence, testing boundaries.

As the evening finally wound to a close and guests began departing for their quarters, Kira caught her father's eye. He gave the slightest nod – he'd seen it too. Tomorrow they would need to talk, to discuss what tonight's gathering had revealed.

But for now, she walked with Henry through the quieting corridors, neither speaking until they were well away from potential eavesdroppers.

"This is bad," Henry said quietly. "The way the prince and Lord Marcus looked at Peek and Aboo... I've seen that look before. When I was a child in Romaland, before I was taken to Latavia as a slave. I saw men look at the market animals the same way."

"Like they were evaluating merchandise," Kira finished grimly.

"Or a menu," Henry corrected. "Kira, in Romaland, trolls aren't companions or heroes. They're... they're exotic delicacies. I'd heard stories, but I always hoped they were exaggerations."

Kira felt cold settle into her bones. "Your father wants us to go to Romaland and spend time with that rude prince. To negotiate with people who might see our friends as food?"

"To negotiate with people who definitely see our friends as food," Henry said. "And possibly see me as a traitor to my blood. And you..."

He didn't finish, but he didn't need to. Kira understood. Her raptor heritage made her doubly vulnerable – she was both "unnatural" by Romalander standards and a royal prize worth capturing.

"We're going anyway," she said finally. "Aren't we?"

Henry's hand found hers in the darkened corridor. "Yes. Because if we don't, they'll take it as weakness. And weakness invites aggression."

"Then we prepare," Kira declared, squeezing his hand before releasing it. "We learn everything we can about Romaland, their customs, their laws, their weaknesses. And we make damn sure that when we ride into their kingdom, we're ready for whatever they throw at us."

As they parted ways for the night, Kira paused at her chamber door. Through the window, she could see the Romalander encampment in the guest quarters courtyard. Fires burned there, and shadows moved in patterns that suggested training exercises rather than rest.

An army didn't train in the middle of a diplomatic mission.

Unless, of course, diplomacy was only a mask for something far more dangerous.

Kira closed her door and began planning for war.

Chapter 2 - Preparing for Diplomacy

The morning after the feast, Kira found herself summoned to her father's private study. It was not like the formal chancery where he conducted official business, but the smaller, warmer room tucked away in the north tower where he could think without the weight of the crown bearing down quite so heavily. Kira thought he also used it to get some time away from Queen Selina, who tended to treat her husband the same as she did her young son, Prince Alec.

King Phillip stood at the window when she entered, his hands clasped behind his back, watching the Romalander delegation's morning activities in the courtyard below. He didn't turn as she closed the door, but his voice carried clearly into the quiet room.

"Tell me what you observed last night."

"Other than a prince rudely walking out of a dinner?"

Kira moved to stand beside him, following his gaze. The Romalanders were already up and active, despite the late hour of the feast's end.

"Yes, he is missing this morning, and I'm told he rode home with only a few knights after he walked out," Kira added as they both stared out the window.

Lord Marcus stood in the center of a group of soldiers, gesturing as if giving orders.

"They eat noble creatures," she said bluntly. "Or at least, they brought provisions that smell like thinking and talking animals. Peek's nose doesn't lie."

"No," King Phillip agreed quietly. "Trolls have excellent senses. I noticed Lord Marcus didn't actually deny it."

"He didn't need to. The way he looked at Peek and Aboo told me everything." Kira turned to face her father. "You're still sending us to Romaland? Even knowing what they are?"

"Especially knowing what they are," King Phillip replied, finally meeting her eyes. His face looked older than it had yesterday, worry etching new lines around his eyes. "Kira, Lord Marcus's delegation isn't here to negotiate peace. Prince William didn't come here for dinner. They were here to assess our strengths and weaknesses, to see if Latavia is worth conquering or if it would be easier to simply... contain us."

The king put his arm around Kira. "Maybe even eat some of us," he added.

The words hung in the air like a sword point. Contain. Eat. As if Latavia were a threat to be managed or provide food during lean winters rather than a neighboring kingdom to be respected.

"Then we're walking into a trap," Kira argued.

"Perhaps," King Phillip acknowledged. "But it's a trap we must spring if we're to have any chance of preventing a war we're not ready to fight. The Romalanders grow bolder every year. Their borders press closer. It is only their civil war between North and South Romaland that keeps them at bay. But when Prince Alec is grown and he unites them..."

"Their raids into our border villages increase," Kira interrupted. "It is time to crush them!"

"No, if we don't establish diplomatic relations now, with the North, and on our terms, they'll establish military ones later, on theirs."

Kira wanted to argue, to insist there had to be another way. But she'd sat through enough strategy sessions to know the truth – sometimes the choice wasn't between good options and bad ones, but between terrible options and catastrophic ones.

"What do you need me to do?" she asked.

Pride flashed across her father's face, though his expression remained serious. "You and Henry will lead the diplomatic mission to Prince William's court in North Romaland. Officially, you're there to negotiate a formal peace treaty between all the kingdoms. Unofficially..."

He pulled a rolled parchment from his desk and handed it to her. "I need intelligence. Troop movements, fortifications, supply lines. Evidence of their military preparations. Are the south and north still enemies? Anything that will help us understand what we're truly facing."

"Especially information about Prince William?"

"My spies tell me that King Stephen could die any day. Our peace was due to the treaty I had with King Stephen, under which Prince Alec lived under my protection.

Kira unrolled the parchment, scanning the detailed questions listed there. Her father had been thorough – these weren't casual observations, but the kind of military intelligence that could mean the difference between victory and defeat.

"You're asking me to spy on them while negotiating with them."

"I'm asking you to survive while protecting your kingdom," King Phillip corrected gently. "The North Romalanders will be doing the same. Lord Marcus has probably already composed three reports about our defenses, our food stores, our military readiness. Prince William used Peek and Aboo's appearance as an excuse to ride home the long way. This is how the war game is played, Kira. The only question is whether we play it well enough to avoid war."

"And if we can't?" Kira asked quietly.

"Then we prepare to fight a war we have very little chance of winning," her father replied with devastating honesty. "North and South Romaland have five times our population, three times our standing army, and resources we can only dream of. Our only advantages are the forbidden lands – which they fear and keep the north and south apart – and the fact that we've never lost a defensive war on our own soil."

"Defense, a wise ruler only thinks of defense, not of war," Kira repeated the words. These words her mother had taught her. Defense prioritizes protecting what exists rather than destroying what others have built. It's fundamentally about preservation—of lives, infrastructure, relationships, and resources—rather than devastation.

When Kira thought about this, she felt the weight of responsibility settle onto her shoulders. This wasn't just a diplomatic mission. It was potentially the key to Latavia's survival, and the survival of all species.

"I'll need time to prepare. To study their customs, their language, their..."

"You'll have three days," King Phillip interrupted. "Lord Marcus's delegation departs in four, and you need to travel with them. It's the only way to ensure your safe passage through Romalander territory."

"Three days?" Kira's voice rose despite her best efforts. "To prepare for a mission this important?"

"I know." Her father's expression was painful. "It's not enough. It's nowhere near enough. But it's what we have." He placed both hands on her shoulders, his grip firm and warm. "I wouldn't send you if I didn't believe you could do this. You're your mother's daughter, Kira. You have her strength, her intelligence, and her ability to see through lies to the truth beneath. You also have something she never did – a true friend who will stand with you no matter what."

As if summoned by the mention, a knock sounded at the door. King Phillip called out permission to enter, and Henry stepped inside, looking freshly scrubbed and alert despite the late night.

"Sir Henry," King Phillip greeted him formally. "Thank you for joining us. Please, sit." He gestured to the chairs arranged around a small table near the fireplace, and they all settled in. "I've been briefing Princess Kira on the true nature of your upcoming mission to Romaland."

Henry's jaw tightened almost imperceptibly. "We're being sent to spy on Prince William while pretending to negotiate peace."

"Bluntly put, but accurate," King Phillip confirmed. "I won't insult your intelligence by pretending otherwise. This will be dangerous, possibly more dangerous than your and Kira's quest to the forbidden lands to save Prince Alec. You'll be surrounded by people who view compassion as weakness and strength as the right to dominate others. You'll need to smile and bow to nobles who might be planning your deaths. And worst of all, you'll need to do it while appearing grateful for their hospitality."

"Sounds delightful," Kira muttered.

A ghost of a smile crossed her father's face. "The life of a diplomat rarely is." His expression sobered again. "Henry, I need to ask you something, and I need you to answer honestly. Will returning to Romaland... will it compromise your judgment? Your loyalty?"

Henry met the king's gaze steadily. "When Nesta was here, she promised to do some research. I received a letter a few months ago. Romaland tossed me away as a child after Latavia knights killed whatever family I had.

As an orphan in Romaland, they would have worked me to death as the lowest class of humans if Latavian soldiers hadn't raided the camp where I was held. I owe Romaland nothing but the memory of pain. My loyalty is to you, to Kira, and to this kingdom. Always."

"I had to ask," King Phillip said gently. "Not because I doubted you, but because you needed to say it aloud. You need to remind yourself when things become difficult." He pulled out another rolled parchment. "I have a secondary objective for you specifically, Henry. I want you to search for any records of your family, your origins. Prince William may use your class and heritage as leverage or temptation. I'd rather you know the truth before he has the chance to weaponize it."

Kira watched Henry's face carefully. She knew how much the mystery of his origins haunted him – the lack of family, of history, of knowing where he truly came from. Her father was offering him something precious, but also potentially dangerous.

"Thank you, Your Majesty," Henry said quietly. "I'll search carefully. But I won't let personal concerns distract from the mission."

"I know you won't," King Phillip replied. "That's why I trust you with this." He stood, and they rose with him. "You have three days to prepare. Nesta will brief you on Romalander customs and geography. She's the only person we have with recent direct knowledge of their court. Use that time wisely."

"Nesta is here?" The king and Henry looked at Kira. They both knew the reason why nobody had told her. Kira was jealous of the beautiful Nesta.

While in the enchanted forest, she was certain that there was an attraction between Henry and Nesta that was deeper than them both being Romalanders. Nobody wanted to bring Kira's wrath of jealousy to the surface. The king waved a hand of dismissal, but as they left the king's study, Kira grabbed Henry's arm, pulling him into an alcove off the main corridor. "Why didn't you tell me about Nesta? Are you really ready for this? To go back to the place where you were enslaved?"

Henry was quiet for a long moment, his eyes distant. "No," he finally admitted. "I don't think I'll ever be ready. But I'm less afraid of going back than I am of what happens if we don't. Lord Marcus looked at Peek and Aboo like they were livestock, Kira. If that's how they view beings they consider beneath them, imagine what they're planning for kingdoms they want to conquer."

"Then we don't let them conquer anything," Kira said fiercely. "We go, we smile, we learn everything we can, and we come back with enough intelligence to protect our home."

"Simple," Henry said with a wry smile.

"I never said it would be simple," Kira shot back. "I said we'd do it. There's a difference." She released his arm and straightened her tunic. "Come on. If we only have three days, we'd better start with Nesta. The faster we learn what passes for manners in Romaland, the less likely I am to accidentally start a war by insulting some pompous lord."

"You? Insult someone?" Henry's smile widened. "That's completely unprecedented!"

Kira punched his arm – not hard, but enough to make her point. As they walked toward the east tower where Nesta kept her maps and records when she visited, Kira tried not to think about what might be waiting for them in Romaland. She tried not to think about the beautiful Nesta. Better to focus on what she could control: preparation, training, and making sure that when they rode into enemy territory, they were as ready as three days could make them.

♠

They found Nesta exactly where they expected – bent over her worktable, surrounded by maps and documents, her dark hair pinned up with what appeared to be spare quills. She looked up as they entered, and her face brightened with a warm smile.

"Kira! Henry! I heard about your mission. I arrived this morning, and I've been preparing materials."

She gestured to the organized chaos spread across every available surface. "Maps of Romaland's territories, trade routes, notable families, cultural customs – I've compiled everything I could think of."

"This morning?" Kira asked, noting the dark circles under Nesta's eyes. "You made good time... from Romaland."

"No, I was in the enchanted forest, perfecting my maps and traveled through the night when the knights came to fetch me."

When did you sleep?" Henry asked with concern.

Nesta waved him off. "Sleep can wait. This is important." She pulled out a large map, spreading it across the main table and weighing down the corners with ink bottles. "First, geography. North and South Romaland are roughly three times the size of Latavia, but much of that land is agricultural plains and in the South. The North's population is concentrated in five major villages, with Prince William's capital here." She tapped a spot on the eastern edge of the map.

Henry leaned over the map, studying it intently. "I remember some of this from your letters."

"Letters?" Kira asked as she noticed a blush marching across Henry's face.

"The slave camp where I was held was... somewhere in this region." He indicated a spot west of the capital.

"That was thirteen years ago," Nesta said gently. "The landscape has changed. Prince William has been aggressive about expansion and development. But the basic geography remains the same." She pulled out another document. "Now, customs. This is where things get complicated."

"How complicated?" Kira asked warily.

"Very," Nesta replied. "Romalander society is rigidly hierarchical. Everyone and everything has a specific place, and stepping outside that place is considered not just rude, but dangerous. They categorize all beings into two groups: those with the right to rule, and those whose purpose is to serve or be consumed."

"Consumed?" Henry's voice was flat.

Nesta hesitated, glancing between them. "You need to understand their philosophy. Romalanders believe that strength gives the right to dominate, and that domination can take many forms. For humans of sufficient rank, it means political and military power. For humans of lower rank, it means serving those above them. And for non-humans, or humans with... unusual traits..." She looked meaningfully at Kira. "It means they exist at the pleasure of their betters, to be used however those betters see fit."

"Including as food," Kira finished grimly.

"Including as food," Nesta confirmed. "Though they're somewhat hypocritical about it. They consider consuming normal animals perfectly acceptable, even commendable. But consuming beings that can speak, that can think and reason? That's reserved for special occasions, and it's meant to demonstrate the ultimate form of dominance – not just defeating an enemy, but quite literally consuming them."

Henry had gone pale. "When I was a small child, I remember seeing cages in the market. I thought they held animals for butchering. But some of them... the creatures inside looked at me. They had eyes that understood."

"I'm sorry," Nesta said softly. "I wish I could tell you that you were wrong, that it was your childish imagination. But trolls, talking animals, forest sprites and fairies – in Romaland, these are considered exotic delicacies for the wealthy and powerful. The rarer the creature, the higher the status of the person who serves it at their table."

Kira felt sick. "And we're going into a kingdom where my best friends could be captured and eaten, where my own heritage could make me a target, where Henry might be seen as a traitor for choosing us over them."

"Yes," Nesta said simply. "Which is why you need to understand their rules, their customs, their way of thinking. The only way to survive Romaland is to appear to accept their philosophy while working against it. You have to make them believe you respect their power while secretly documenting their cruelties."

She pulled out another document, this one covered in dense text. "These are their laws regarding non-humans. Study them carefully. Every sentence contains traps. For example, any creature deemed 'unnatural' by Romalander standards can be claimed as property by any noble who encounters it. That includes talking animals, magical beings, and..." She paused meaningfully. "Anyone with non-human ancestry."

"Anyone with raptor blood," Kira translated. "They could claim I'm 'unnatural' and attempt to cage me."

"If they knew about your heritage, yes," Nesta confirmed. "Which is why you absolutely cannot reveal your wings under any circumstances. In Latavia, your mother's lineage is a secret to protect her memory and your throne. In Romaland, it would be a death sentence – or worse, a sentence to become someone's prized possession."

Henry moved to stand beside Kira, his presence solid and reassuring. "We won't let that happen."

"You might not have a choice," Nesta said bluntly. "I'm not trying to frighten you, I'm trying to prepare you. Romaland is nothing like Latavia. The rules you've grown up with, the values you hold dear – none of that matters there. Honor is weakness. Compassion is foolishness. Might makes right, and the strong owe nothing to the weak except dominion."

"Then how do we negotiate with people like that?" Kira demanded. "How do we find common ground with a kingdom that views half the world as potential livestock?"

"You don't find common ground," Nesta replied. "You find leverage. You identify what they want and what they fear, and you use both to create a situation where peace serves their interests better than war. It won't be a peace based on mutual respect or shared values. It'll be a peace based on cold calculation of benefit and risk."

Kira hated everything about this. Hated the necessity of playing diplomatic games with people she wanted to fight. Hated that her father was right about needing this intelligence. Hated that the price of Latavia's safety might be smiling at monsters while they discussed eating her friends. Hated the way Henry looked at Nesta.

But she was her mother's daughter, as King Phillip had said. And her mother had taught her that sometimes the bravest thing a warrior could do was sheath their sword and fight with words instead.

"All right," she said, pulling up a chair. "Teach us. Everything. We have three days to become experts on a culture we despise. Let's get started."

Nesta's smile was proud and sad at the same time. "I'll make tea. This is going to take a while."

♠

As they dove into the intensive study of Romalander customs, none of them noticed a small green figure hiding in the corner behind a stack of rolled maps. Freddy the Frog had followed Henry from the courtyard that morning, curious about where his favorite human was going in such a hurry. Now, crouched in the shadows and struggling to keep his natural scream reflex under control, he listened to every word about the kingdom where creatures like him were considered delicacies.

His large eyes grew wider with each revelation. The slave markets. The cages in the town square. The special occasions where talking creatures were the centerpiece of elaborate feasts.

The laws that stripped any being deemed "unnatural" of all rights and protections.

Freddy's mind raced. He'd thought Latavia was strange enough, with its mix of accepting some magical creatures while being wary of others. But Romaland sounded like a nightmare – a place where being able to talk and think didn't make you a person, it just made you more interesting to eat.

And Kira and Henry were going there. Walking right into that horror, supposedly to negotiate peace.

But Freddy had excellent hearing, and he'd caught the things they weren't saying aloud. This wasn't just about negotiation. This was about war. About Romaland's plans to conquer Latavia. About the fact that if this mission failed, the enchanted forest and all its inhabitants might face the same fate as those creatures in the Romalander markets.

Freddy knew he should leave, should hop away to the enchanted forest before they spotted him and asked what he was doing there. But something kept him frozen in place, listening to every word, storing every detail about the kingdom that might soon become a threat to everything and everyone he cared about.

When the lesson finally paused for a break, Freddy quietly slipped out through a crack in the wall, his heart pounding with fear and a growing sense that maybe – just maybe – knowing all this information meant he had a responsibility to do something about it.

Even if doing something meant facing the very creatures who viewed frogs like him as appetizers.

Freddy hopped through the castle corridors, his mind spinning with possibilities. He needed to find Peek and Aboo. The trolls needed to know what they were walking into. He had heard the twins talking about ignoring Kira's order to stay home.

But as he rounded a corner, he nearly collided with a pair of expensive boots. Freddy looked up – and up, and up – into the cold, appraising eyes of Lord Marcus himself.

The Romalander ambassador smiled, and it was not a pleasant expression.

"Well, well," Lord Marcus purred. "What have we here? A screaming frog, loose in the castle and so far from the enchanted forest. How... convenient." He crouched down, moving with the fluid grace of a predator. "I wonder what interesting things you might have overheard, little morsel. Not that it matters. Even if you could warn them, would they believe a frog?"

Freddy's throat convulsed with the urge to scream, but terror froze the sound in his chest. Lord Marcus reached out one gloved hand, his smile widening.

"Perhaps I'll keep you," he mused. "A little taste of home while we're trapped in this barbaric kingdom that treats food as friends." His fingers closed around Freddy's body, lifting him off the ground. "Don't worry. I'll make sure you're... well-seasoned."

Freddy finally found his voice. The scream that erupted from his throat was deafening, echoing off the stone walls with enough force to rattle the windows. Lord Marcus cursed and dropped him, clapping his hands over his ears.

Freddy hit the floor running – or hopping, rather – and disappeared into the nearest crack in the wall, his heart hammering so hard he thought it might burst. Behind him, he heard Lord Marcus shouting for servants, but Freddy was already gone, racing through the secret passages that only small creatures knew existed.

He had to warn Peek and Aboo, because whatever Kira and Henry were preparing for, Freddy had a terrible feeling it was going to be much, much worse than they imagined.

By the time evening fell on that first day of preparation, Kira's head was spinning with information. Romalander greeting protocols (different for each rank and station). Dietary customs (don't ask what's in anything). Rules about eye contact (maintain it with superiors, avoid it with inferiors, and never, ever let them see you flinch). The hierarchy of nobles (Prince William at the top, then his council of five lords, then military commanders like knights, then wealthy merchants, then common humans, then non-humans who were considered "tame," and finally non-humans who were considered "wild" – which meant fair game for anyone).

"I need to practice," Kira announced, standing up from the table where they'd been studying. "My head's too full. I need to move, to fight, to do something physical, or I'm going to explode."

Henry nodded, understanding. "The training yard?"

"The training yard," Kira confirmed. "But not the main one. Too many prying eyes." She glanced meaningfully toward the window, where the Romalander delegation's quarters were visible. "The private one behind the armory."

They found the small training yard empty, as expected. This was where the royal family practiced when they wanted privacy – a walled courtyard with well-maintained equipment and enough space to move freely without an audience.

Kira selected two practice swords from the rack, tossing one to Henry. He caught it easily, testing its weight and balance with the automatic movements of someone who'd trained with weapons since childhood.

They squared off without discussion, falling into the familiar rhythm of sparring partners who knew each other's moves intimately. Kira attacked first, a high slash that Henry ducked easily. He countered with a low sweep that she jumped over, spinning to bring her blade toward his ribs.

For several minutes, they simply fought – not the careful, technical practice they did with other knights, but the full-force combat they only dared attempt with each other. Each knew the other's limits, trusted the other's control, and pushed just hard enough to make it real without making it dangerous.

Kira felt some of the tension drain from her shoulders as she moved, her body remembering lessons her mind couldn't articulate. This was what she was good at. This was what made sense. Not diplomatic niceties or cultural sensitivities, but the honest simplicity of blade against blade, skill against skill.

"You're holding back," Henry observed, catching her blade and holding it locked against his own.

"I'm not," Kira protested.

"You are." Henry pushed her blade away and stepped back, lowering his weapon. "You're afraid."

The word stung because it was true. Kira lowered her own sword, breathing hard. "I'm afraid of going to a place where I can't be myself. Where I have to watch every word and pretend to respect people who view my friends as food. I'm afraid of failing my father, of making a mistake that starts a war, of getting you killed because I can't control my temper."

"Kira..."

"I'm afraid," she continued, the words tumbling out now that she'd started, "that when we get to Romaland, they'll see through me. They'll know I'm different, that I'm hiding something, and they'll use it against us. Against Latavia. I'm afraid that all the training in the world won't be enough because I'm not my mother. I can't do what she did – hide in plain sight, smile at enemies, play political games. I'm a warrior, Henry. I fight with swords, not words."

Henry set down his practice blade and moved to stand in front of her. "You think your mother wasn't afraid? She was part raptor in a kingdom that had just outlawed raptors. She lived every day knowing that if anyone discovered the truth, she'd lose everything; her position, her family, possibly her life. And she did it anyway, because that's what courage is. Not the absence of fear but doing what must be done despite the fear."

"That's different," Kira argued weakly.

"It's not," Henry said firmly. "Kira, you're the bravest person I know. You faced down twin trolls armed with nothing but wit. You crossed a poisoned bridge that terrified experienced knights. You befriended creatures that others called monsters. You've already been doing the hard thing your whole life – choosing compassion over convention, friendship over fear. Romaland is just another challenge. A bigger one, yes. A more dangerous one, absolutely. But you've never backed down from a challenge yet."

Kira wanted to believe him. Wanted to feel the confidence in his words settling into her bones, replacing the anxiety that had taken up residence there.

"What if I make a mistake?" she asked quietly.

"Then we fix it," Henry replied simply. "Together. That's what we do, Kira. We face impossible things, survive them, and come out stronger. This won't be different."

"Promise?" The word came out smaller than she intended, more vulnerable.

Henry smiled, the same smile he'd given her years ago, when he was just a slave boy with a wooden horse and she was a princess who didn't know how to play. "Promise," he said. "Now come on. We have two more days to prepare, and I intend to spend at least some of that time making sure you can insult a Romalander noble in their own language without them realizing they've been insulted."

Despite everything, Kira laughed. "Is that a skill Nesta taught you?"

"No," Henry admitted. "But I figure we'll need it eventually, so we might as well start developing it now."

They gathered up their practice weapons and headed back toward the castle proper, their conversation shifting to lighter topics – strategies for enduring boring diplomatic dinners, bets on which Romalander would insult them first, speculations about whether the castle's cook could possibly make veggie dishes look appealing enough to satisfy their guests.

Neither of them noticed the shadow watching from the castle tower above. Lord Marcus observed the two young people who would soon be his guests in Romaland. He'd learned much from watching them spar. The girl was skilled but emotional, prone to aggressive attacks when frustrated. The boy was more controlled, more defensive, more thoughtful in his approach. He was a Romalander.

But both would be easy to manipulate in different ways.

Lord Marcus smiled. Prince William would be pleased with his report. These Latavians were children playing at diplomacy, sheep walking willingly into the wolf's den.

And when the time came, they would make excellent examples of what happened to kingdoms that defied Romaland's vision of proper order.

He had three more days to prepare as well. Three days to lay the groundwork for the trap that would snap shut the moment Kira and Henry crossed into Romalander territory.

It would be almost too easy.

Chapter 3 - Journey to Romaland

The morning of departure arrived too quickly and not quickly enough. Kira stood in the castle courtyard watching servants load the final supplies onto the diplomatic party's wagons.

Three days of intensive preparation had left her mind crammed with information about Romalander customs, politics, and geography. She could recite the names of Prince William's five councils, explain the proper greeting for seventeen ranks of nobility, and identify regional variations in the Romalander dialect. What she couldn't do was shake the feeling that none of it would be enough.

"Ready?" Henry appeared on her elbow, dressed in traveling clothes that looked both casual and diplomatic.

"No," Kira admitted. "But I don't think more time would help. I'd just find new things to worry about."

Henry's mouth quirked in a half-smile. "That's the most honest thing you've said in three days."

"I've been honest," Kira protested.

"You've been diplomatic," Henry corrected. "It's not the same thing." He glanced around to ensure they weren't overheard, then lowered his voice. "Promise me something. Once we cross into Romaland, once we're surrounded by people we can't trust, promise that with me at least, you'll stay honest. I need to know what you're really thinking, not what you think you should say."

Kira met his eyes, ready for fight, but then she softened. He was just as afraid as she was, just better at hiding it. "I promise. The same goes for you. Whatever happens in Romaland, whatever you discover about your family or your past, don't hide it from me to protect me or because you think I won't understand."

"Deal," Henry agreed, extending his hand. They shook on it, a gesture that felt odd. For a moment, she leaned toward him and closed her eyes. But then she jerked to reality when she heard footsteps.

"Princess Kira! Sir Henry!" Nesta hurried across the courtyard, her arms full of scrolls and maps. "Last-minute preparations. I've marked the safe houses on this map – they're encoded, so if the Romalanders find it, they won't know what they're looking at. These trees here," she pointed to seemingly identical trees.

But Kira noticed some of the trees had an extra branch. "So these trees indicate places where your underground network has safe contacts and shelter," Kira said as she studied the map, memorizing the location of the "different" trees.

"Underground network?" Henry asks.

"People who reject Romalander values," Nesta explained quietly. "Humans who refuse to participate in their cultural cruelties, refugees who've escaped their classifications. They operate in secret, helping creatures flee to safer kingdoms. If you encounter them, they might be willing to provide information or assistance."

Nesta handed over another scroll. "And this contains everything I could learn about Prince William's court in the past year. New appointments, political alliances, rumors of conflict. Read it carefully once you're safely away from the delegation."

"Thank you," Kira said, meaning it. "For everything. For the information, for the preparation, for caring enough to help us."

Nesta's smile was warm but tinged with worry. "Just come back safely. Both of you. Latavia needs you more than you know."

Lord Marcus's voice carried across the courtyard, sharp and commanding. "The delegation departs in ten minutes. Anyone not in position will be left behind."

"That's our cue," Henry muttered. He offered Kira his arm in the formal manner appropriate for a knight escorting a princess, and she took it, straightening her spine and lifting her chin. Time to put on the diplomatic mask and pray it didn't slip at the wrong moment.

The diplomatic party was impressive in size. Lord Marcus had brought twenty Romalander guards, plus servants, advisors, and enough wagons to supply a small army. The Latavian delegation was much smaller by necessity: Kira and Henry as the primary diplomats, six knights as their honor guard, and three servants to manage their supplies and tend their camp. Henry glanced back at Peek and Aboo. They had dressed in his green tunic colors for today and obviously wanted to come along, but Nesta's notes clearly indicated that trolls were hated in Romaland.

King Phillip and Queen Selina stood at the castle gates to see them off. The formal farewell was brief but weighed with unspoken concerns. When Kira's father embraced her, he whispered in her ear, "Trust your instincts. If something feels wrong, it probably is. Don't sacrifice yourself trying to maintain diplomatic niceties."

"I won't," Kira whispered back, though she wasn't entirely sure it was a promise she could keep.

The journey began with uncomfortable civility. Lord Marcus rode at the head of the column, his posture radiating authority and disdain in equal measure. The Romalander guards kept to themselves, speaking in low voices and casting suspicious glances at their Latavian companions. The Latavian knights responded with careful politeness and hands that never strayed far from their weapons.

Kira and Henry rode in the middle of the formation, positioned where they could observe both groups. The arrangement felt deliberately symbolic – trapped between Latavia and Romaland, caught in the middle of tensions they were supposedly meant to resolve.

The first day passed in tense silence, broken only by necessary communication about pace and rest stops. They made camp that night still within Latavian territory, close enough to the border that everyone could feel it looming ahead like a physical barrier.

As the servants set up tents and prepared the evening meal, Kira noticed the Romalanders had once again brought out their mysterious provisions. The smell that wafted from their cooking fires was distinctive and unsettling – preserved meat with an almost sweet undertone that made her stomach turn.

"Don't stare," Henry murmured, coming to stand beside her. "They know it bothers us. That's part of why they do it."

"It's not just that it bothers me," Kira replied quietly. "It's that they're so casual about it. As if there's nothing wrong with what they're eating, as if the idea that it might have been a thinking, feeling creature doesn't even occur to them."

"Because to them, it doesn't matter," Henry said. "In Romalander philosophy, being able to think just makes you more interesting prey. It doesn't grant you rights or protection. Strength grants rights. Power grants rights. Everything else is just... resources to be used by those strong enough to claim them."

Before Kira could respond, two Latavian knights approached – James and Mark. It was a natural reflex for Kira to put her hand on her sword. A few years ago, they had betrayed her and joined forces with King Stephen to united North and South Romaland and take over Latavia. They had killed King Alexander of the South and his wife, Queen Selina, had sought asylum in Latavia. To protect the heir to the South's throne, Kira's father had married Selina and raised Prince Alec as his son. But there was a time when everyone thought Kira was the traitor and one thing she learned, Latavians believed in truth and forgiveness. James and Mark joined Henry's quest into the enchanted forest, and Kira learned to trust them again.

"Princess, we've secured the perimeter. No signs of trouble, but several of us noticed movement in the forest. Could be animals, could be something else."

"Something else?" Kira asked.

Mark glanced toward the darkening tree line. "Refugees, maybe. People fleeing Romaland. The closer we get to the border, the more likely we are to encounter them. They tend to travel at night, trying to avoid Romalander patrols."

A commotion from the forest edge interrupted their conversation. Several Romalander guards had drawn their weapons, shouting in their harsh dialect and gesturing toward the trees. Lord Marcus strode over, his face thunderous.

"What's the meaning of this?" he demanded.

One of his guards responded in Romalander, too quickly for Kira to fully catch. But she understood enough – they'd spotted movement, possibly refugees, possibly creatures fleeing across the border.

"Stand down," Lord Marcus ordered. His guard protested, and Lord Marcus's voice grew colder. "I said, stand down. We're still in Latavian territory. These creatures, whatever they are, are under King Phillip's protection until we cross the border. After that..." He smiled unpleasantly. "After that, they'll learn what happens to those who flee Romaland's rightful authority."

The guards lowered their weapons reluctantly, but Kira could see them watching the tree line with predatory interest. As darkness fully fell, she kept her own watch, trying to spot whatever had caught their attention.

There – a flicker of movement between the trees. And another. Shapes that could have been deer or wild boar, except for the way they moved with cautious intelligence, keeping to the shadows, clearly aware they were being watched.

Henry must have seen them too, because he touched her arm gently. "Don't interfere," he said quietly. "Not yet. We're not even in Romaland yet, and already we're being tested. They want to see if we'll object, if we'll try to protect refugees. It'll tell them how soft we are, how easily manipulated."

"So, we just let them hunt thinking creatures?" Kira hissed.

"We let them show their hand," Henry corrected. "We observe, we remember, and we use it later when we have leverage. That's what your father would do."

Kira hated it, but he was right. She forced herself to turn away from the tree line, to walk back to the Latavian section of camp and focus on more immediate concerns. But she made note of every guard who'd shown particular eagerness, every Romalander who'd looked at those fleeing shapes with hunger rather than concern.

Intelligence gathering for Kira had started now.

♠

The second day brought them to the border itself, marked by a massive stone pillar carved with both Latavian and Romalander symbols. On the Latavian side, the inscription read: "Peace

between peoples, respect for all who dwell within our borders."
On the Romalander side: "Strength preserves order, order
preserves civilization."

The philosophical difference couldn't have been clearer.

As they crossed into Romaland, Kira felt something shift in the
atmosphere. It wasn't physical, exactly, but she could sense it – a
change in how the Romalander guards carried themselves, a new
tension in how they looked at the Latavian party. They were on
home ground now, and everyone knew it.

The landscape itself seemed to reflect the cultural differences.
Where Latavia had allowed its forests to grow wild and free,
Romaland had imposed order. Trees grew in neat rows, cultivated
and pruned. Fields stretched in geometric precision. Even the
roads were wider, straighter, more aggressively maintained than
their Latavian counterparts.

It was impressive. It was also deeply unsettling, this
determination to control and shape everything according to
human design.

They encountered their first village by mid-afternoon. It was
larger and more prosperous-looking than most Latavian villages,
with well-maintained buildings and busy market squares. But as
they rode through, Kira noticed details that made her skin crawl.

Cages. Small ones stacked at the edge of the market, each
containing creatures that ranged from recognizable animals to
things she'd never seen before. And some of those creatures
looked at her as the party passed, their eyes too intelligent, too
aware, to be mere animals.

"Don't look," Henry warned. "And definitely don't stop. That
market is legal here, sanctioned by their laws. If you object, you'll
insult their culture and give them leverage against us."

Kira forced her gaze forward, but she couldn't block out the
sounds – the chittering, chirping, and occasional clear words
coming from those cages. "Help me," one voice said, barely
audible over the market noise. "Please, someone help me."

Her hands tightened on her reins hard enough that her knuckles went white. Julius, her horse, sensed her distress and tossed his head nervously.

"Steady," Henry said, his own voice tight with controlled emotion. "We can't save them all. Not now. But we can remember. We can document. And we can use that information to build a case for why Latavia should never, ever become like this."

The village finally fell behind them, but the memory of those cages lingered. That night, when they made camp, Kira pulled out one of the blank journals Nesta had given her and began to write. She documented everything – the location of the village, the size of the market, the number and types of creatures she'd seen imprisoned. If Latavia needed evidence of Romalander cruelty, she would provide it in excruciating detail.

As she wrote by firelight, a sound from the darkness made her look up. There, just beyond the ring of firelight, a pair of large eyes reflected the flames. Not human eyes. Not quite animal eyes either.

The eyes, whatever or whoever it was, studied her for a long moment, then deliberately stepped into the light. It was a badger, but larger than any badger Kira had ever seen, with silver streaks in its fur and an expression of profound weariness on its whiskered face.

"Princess Kira of Latavia," the badger said in a voice like rustling leaves. "I am Arnold, and I bring a warning from those who still value freedom over survival."

Kira glanced around quickly, but the Romalanders were occupied with their own camp and the Latavian guards were stationed too far away to overhear. She gestured for the badger to come closer, keeping her voice low. "You're taking a terrible risk coming here. If they see you..."

"They'll cage me for their next feast, I know," Arnold interrupted. "But some risks are worth taking. You travel into the heart of darkness, young princess, into a kingdom where creatures like me exist only to serve or to be served at the table. You must understand what you face."

"I've seen the markets," Kira said grimly.

"Markets are nothing," Arnold replied. "They're symptoms of a larger disease. Prince William isn't content with maintaining Romaland's current practices. He's expanding them. New laws that strip more rights from more beings. Hunting parties that range farther and farther into the wild places. Bounties on any creature deemed 'unnatural' by his ever-broader definitions."

"Unnatural," Kira repeated. "Like creatures with wings?"

Arnold's dark eyes held hers. "Like creatures with wings. Like anyone with mixed heritage. Like those who dare to help the persecuted flee to safer lands. Prince William's vision isn't just for Romaland, Princess. He believes all kingdoms should adopt his philosophy. He sees Latavia's tolerance as weakness, as a corruption that must be cleansed."

"He wants to conquer us, and his father tried before. His father, King Stephen murdered King Alexander, my step-brother's father. They came from the South and have made it hard for you?" Kira said, though it wasn't really a question.

"Worse," Arnold replied. "He wants to remake you. To force Latavia to adopt Romalander values, to turn your kingdom into another province where the strong devour the weak and call it civilization."

Arnold's whiskers twitched nervously. "There's something else. Prince William has been getting closer to our network. Three safe houses were discovered last month. Two more went silent last week. Elena thinks we still have time, but..." He paused meaningfully. "Be very careful who you trust, even among the resistance. Fear makes people do terrible things."

The badger moved closer, his voice dropping even lower. "And he has a particular interest in you, Princess. He knows what you are, what you hide. The underground has ears everywhere, including in his court, and they've heard him speak of it. You're not just a diplomat to him. You're a prize. The ultimate proof of his philosophy – a royal raptor, caged and displayed as proof that even the most powerful can be brought low."

Kira felt ice form in her stomach. "How does he know? My heritage is a carefully guarded secret."

"Secrets have a way of spreading when they're valuable enough," Arnold said sadly. "Someone in Latavia sold that information to him. We don't know who, but the damage is done. Prince William invited your diplomatic mission specifically to bring you within his reach as King Stephen's health continues to decline. The treaty negotiations are a facade. The moment you enter the Romaland castle, you'll be walking into a trap designed specifically for you."

"Then I won't go," Kira said immediately. "We'll turn back, tell my father..."

"And Prince William will call it cowardice and use it as justification for invasion," Arnold interrupted. "You're trapped, Princess. If you advance, you risk capture. If you retreat, you guarantee war. The only path forward is to go, knowing the danger, and be clever enough to spring the trap without getting caught in it."

"How?" Kira demanded. "How do I outsmart someone who knows my secrets, holds all the power in his own kingdom, and has already planned for my arrival?"

Arnold was quiet for a moment, his whiskers twitching thoughtfully. "You remind him that strength isn't just about power, it's about knowing when to use it and when to withhold it. You make him believe you're valuable alive rather than caged. And remember... you're not alone. The underground network exists throughout Romaland, people and creatures who reject these cruelties. Find them. Trust them. Let them help you."

"How will I know them?" Kira asked.

"Look for the gold feather," Arnold said. "Worn as jewelry, carved into doorframes, drawn in the corners of maps. It's our symbol, our sign that a place or person believes in the old ways, when all creatures were judged by their deeds rather than their species." He began backing away into the darkness. "I must go before I'm spotted. But remember, Princess – you have more allies in North and South Romaland than you know. Some of them are human, some not. All of them committed to resisting Prince William's vision of the future."

"Wait," Kira called softly. "What about you? Where will you go?"

Arnold paused at the edge of the firelight. "Into the deep forests, where Romalander hunters haven't yet learned the paths. I'll survive, Princess. The question is – will you?" He disappeared into the darkness before she could answer.

Kira sat frozen for several heartbeats, her mind racing with implications. Prince William knew about her raptor heritage. This entire diplomatic mission was a trap. Someone in Latavia had betrayed her.

She needed to tell Henry. Needed to tell the Latavian guards. Needed to...

"Interesting conversation," Lord Marcus's voice came from behind her, and Kira's heart stopped.

She turned slowly to find the Romalander lord standing just outside her tent, his expression unreadable in the firelight. How long had he been there? How much had he heard?

"A local badger," Kira said, keeping her voice steady through sheer force of will. "I've always been fascinated by wildlife. In Latavia, we believe all creatures have wisdom to share, if we're willing to listen."

"How... charming," Lord Marcus replied. "In Romaland, we believe that wisdom comes from strength, and strength from decisive action. Badgers are clever creatures, Princess, but they're also notorious liars when cornered. They all call themselves Arnold and are famous for being traitors. I wouldn't put too much faith in anything they say, especially if you give them food."

He moved closer, and Kira's hand instinctively moved toward her sword hilt. Lord Marcus noticed, and his smile widened.

"Jumpy, Princess? There's no need. You're under my protection as part of this diplomatic mission. Nothing will harm you..." He paused deliberately. "Until we reach Prince William's court, and proper hospitality requires he assumes responsibility for your safety."

"And King Stephen?"

"You're lucky he is gravely ill. He'd kill you on sight."

The threat was clear, wrapped in diplomatic language but unmistakable in intent. It appears that the treaty they made with King Stephen to protect Prince Alec was worth less than the paper it was written on.

"I appreciate your protection, Lord Marcus," Kira said, matching his formal tone. "And I look forward to talking to Prince William again and discussing how our kingdoms might find common ground."

"Oh, I'm certain you'll find the prince fascinating, if you don't make him angry," Lord Marcus replied. "He has such interesting ideas about common ground. About natural hierarchies. About ensuring that every creature and every kingdom knows its proper place in the order of things." He bowed slightly. "Sleep well, Princess. We reach Prince William's territory tomorrow, and you'll want to be well-rested for your first glimpse of true Romalander hospitality."

He walked away, leaving Kira staring after him with her heart pounding and her mind racing. She had to find Henry. Had to share Arnold's warning. They had to figure out how they were going to survive walking into a trap when they couldn't afford to turn back.

As she ducked into her tent to find Henry's, a flash of green caught her eye. There, perched on her travel pack, sat Freddy the frog, his large eyes worried.

"Princess," he whispered. "We need to talk about what I've heard. About the fact that if you're walking into danger, maybe you shouldn't walk alone."

Kira stared at him. "Freddy, what are you doing here? This is the worst possible place for a talking frog!"

"I know," Freddy admitted. "That's exactly why I came. Because someone needs to watch out for you, and apparently, frogs are the only ones crazy enough to volunteer for suicide missions." He hopped closer. "Now, are you going to tell Sir Henry what that badger said, or do I need to do it for you?"

"All right," she said quietly. "Let's find Henry. And then we need to figure out how we're going to survive the next few days without getting caged, served at a feast, or starting a war."

"Is that all?" Freddy asked dryly. "And here I thought this was going to be difficult."

Chapter 4 - Entering the Lion's Den

The morning they entered Romaland's territory proper, the landscape changed again. Gone were even the orderly forests and geometric fields of outer Romaland. Here, everything seemed designed to impress and intimidate in equal measure.

The road widened into a grand thoroughfare paved with smooth stones that must have required armies of workers to lay. Marble statues lined the route at regular intervals, each depicting some triumph of Romalander history. But as Kira rode past them, she noticed the themes – humans standing victorious over conquered creatures, warriors with caged beasts at their feet, nobles presiding over scenes of subjugation presented as civilization.

"Subtle," Henry muttered beside her, his eyes tracking the same disturbing imagery.

"That's the point," Kira replied quietly. "They want everyone to know exactly what they value. Power. Dominance. Control." She gestured to a particularly elaborate statue showing what appeared to be a king standing atop a pile of various creatures, his foot planted on the head of something that might have been a troll. "This is what they think civilization looks like."

Lord Marcus, riding ahead, must have heard them. He twisted in his saddle, his smile sharp. "Art that tells truth, Princess. Those statues commemorate King Aldric the Great, who split up Romaland three centuries ago by bringing order to chaos. Before him, all this land was overrun with dangerous creatures that threatened humanity's survival. He established the natural hierarchy that allows civilization to flourish in the North."

"By eliminating anything that didn't fit his vision of natural," Henry said, his voice carefully neutral.

"By establishing proper order in the North and letting creature roam free in the South," Lord Marcus corrected. "Strength at the top, the north, and weakness at the bottom in the south. True threats into the forbidden lands. Everything and everyone in their proper place. It's a system that has brought Romaland three centuries of prosperity and power. Surely even Latavia can appreciate the value of that with your 'enchanted forest' where you banish your undesirables."

Kira bit back the dozen sharp responses that crowded her tongue. This was exactly the kind of test Henry had warned her about – provocations designed to make her reveal her true feelings, to crack her diplomatic mask. She forced a smile that felt like it might shatter her face. "Indeed. Romaland's strength is evident in everything we've seen."

The answer satisfied Lord Marcus enough that he turned back to the road ahead, but Kira caught Henry's concerned glance. She was holding on to her composure by her fingernails, and they both knew it. And they hadn't even reached the castle yet.

As they crested a hill, Prince William's castle came into view, and despite her determination not to be impressed, Kira's breath caught. It was massive, easily three times the size of Castle Latavia, built of dark stone that seemed to absorb light rather than reflect it. Towers rose like accusing fingers toward the sky, each topped with banners bearing the Romalander crest – a crowned eagle clutching a sword in one talon and chains in the other.

The castle walls were thick and high, clearly built as much to intimidate as to defend. But what made Kira's stomach turn were the decorations. More statues, yes, but also what appeared to be actual preserved creatures mounted on the walls like trophies. Wings stretched in permanent flight. Heads frozen in silent roars. Bodies posed in dramatic defeat.

"By all the ancient laws," she whispered, unable to stop herself.

Henry's hand found hers, hidden between their horses, and squeezed tightly. The gesture was brief but steadying. They'd known it would be bad. Arnold had warned them. But knowing and seeing were two very different things.

As they approached the main gates, Kira noticed the village that had grown up around the castle. It was larger than any Latavian settlement except the capital, but the same unsettling elements appeared here too. Cages in the market square, creatures confined and displayed. But here there was also something worse – a platform in the center of the square where what looked like an auction was taking place.

A man in fine robes stood on the platform beside a cage containing something small and trembling. His voice carried across the square as they passed: "Genuine fairy, captured just last week in the northern woods! Excellent for decorative purposes or, for the adventurous host, a truly exotic addition to any feast! Shall we start the bidding at fifty silver pieces?"

Kira's hands tightened on her reins so hard that Julius whinnied in protest. A fairy. They were auctioning off a fairy like it was a particularly interesting piece of livestock.

"Don't look," Henry said urgently. "Kira, don't look. Don't react. We're being watched by dozens of people, and any response you give will be reported back to Prince William within the hour."

But Kira couldn't help herself. She turned toward the platform just in time to see the fairy – small, delicate, with gossamer wings that trembled with fear – meet her eyes. The fairy's mouth opened in what might have been a plea or a warning, but the auctioneer chose that moment to drop a heavy cloth over the cage, cutting off the view.

"Excellent condition, as you can see!" the auctioneer continued. "Wings intact, voice box still functional—"

"Voice box?" Kira hissed to Henry. "They're talking about it like it's a piece of furniture!"

"Because that's how they see it," Henry replied, his own voice tight with suppressed emotion. "Kira, please. We can't save everyone. We can't even save anyone, not yet. But if we blow our cover now, if we reveal how we really feel, we'll be useless for gathering intelligence and we might not survive to make it home to warn your father."

He was right. Kira knew he was right. But knowing didn't make it easier to turn away from that trembling creature in its cage, to pretend she hadn't seen, hadn't cared.

They passed through the castle gates, and Kira felt them close behind her with a finality that made her skin crawl. The courtyard beyond was immaculate – too clean, too orderly, without a single blade of grass out of place. Servants in matching uniforms stood at attention, their faces carefully blank. More guards than Kira could quickly count lined the walls, their armor gleaming and weapons obviously well-maintained.

And waiting at the base of the grand staircase that led to the castle proper stood Prince William himself.

Kira hadn't really looked at him during the few moments he was in Latavia, disguised as a knight. Today, he looked older, harder, more obviously cruel. Prince William appeared to be in his mid-twenties, handsome in a cold sort of way, with perfectly groomed dark hair and clothes that probably cost more than most Latavian families earned in a year. His smile as they approached was charming, welcoming, and absolutely terrifying in its insincerity.

"Princess Kira! Sir Henry!" Prince William's voice was warm, cultured, the voice of someone who'd been trained since birth to command attention and inspire loyalty. "So good to see you again! Welcome to Romaland. I hope your journey was pleasant and that Lord Marcus has been an adequate host."

"More than adequate, Your Highness," Kira replied, dismounting with Henry's assistance. "We're honored by your invitation and grateful for the opportunity to build bridges between our kingdoms."

"Bridges," Prince William repeated, his smile widening. "What a lovely metaphor. I prefer to think of it as establishing proper understanding between neighbors. Come, you must be exhausted from your travels. Let me show you to your quarters, and then perhaps you'd like a tour of the castle? I think you'll find much to admire in how we've organized things here."

He gestured, and servants immediately appeared to take their horses. Kira noticed that the Latavian guards were being separated from them, guided toward what appeared to be barracks near the outer wall. Standard procedure for diplomatic missions, perhaps, but it meant she and Henry would be alone in the castle proper, surrounded by Romalanders with no immediate backup.

Prince William led them up the grand staircase, keeping up a steady stream of pleasant conversation about the architecture, the history of the castle, the various improvements he'd made since inheriting from his father five years ago. His voice was hypnotic, almost, lulling them with normalcy while their eyes registered increasingly disturbing details.

The hallways were lined with display cases. At first glance, they appeared to hold artifacts – weapons, armor, historical documents. But as they passed, Kira realized some of the "artifacts" were creatures. Small ones, perfectly preserved, positioned in lifelike poses behind glass like museum exhibits.

"My collection," Prince William said, noticing her attention. "I've always been fascinated by the diversity of life in our world. Each of these specimens represents a species or individual of particular interest. This one, for example," he gestured to a case containing something that looked like a tiny dragon, "was the last of its kind. Magnificent creature. It took my hunters three years to track it down."

"You killed it?" The words escaped before Kira could stop them.

"I preserved it," Prince William corrected gently. "Left to its own devices, it would have died eventually anyway, and its unique characteristics would have been lost to history. Now it will be remembered forever, a testament to the incredible variety of life that has graced our world." His eyes met Kira's, and there was something predatory in his gaze. "I believe in honoring the remarkable, Princess. In ensuring that the truly special are never forgotten."

The implication hung in the air between them. Kira was remarkable. Kira was special, with her hidden raptor heritage. And Prince William collected special things.

Henry stepped slightly forward, subtly placing himself between Kira and the prince. "The preservation technique is impressive, Your Highness. Is it a Romalander specialty?"

Prince William's attention shifted to Henry, and Kira saw calculation in his expression. "Indeed. We've perfected many arts over the centuries. Preservation of specimens. Classification of species. Determination of which creatures have value and which are merely... disposable." He paused. "Sir Henry. An interesting case, aren't you? Romalander by birth, Latavian by circumstance. Where does your loyalty truly lie, I wonder?"

"With those who freed me from slavery and gave me the chance to be more than property," Henry replied steadily.

"Slavery," Prince William mused. "Such an ugly word for an efficient system. In Romaland, we prefer to think of it as appropriate placement according to natural ability and worth. Some are born to rule. Some are born to serve. Some are born to be... utilized. Fighting against one's natural place only creates unhappiness."

"And who decides what's natural?" Kira asked, unable to help herself. "Who determines which beings deserve rights and which deserve to be in cages?"

Prince William's smile didn't waver, but his eyes grew colder. "Why, those with the strength to make such decisions, of course. The strong define what is natural. The weak accept those definitions. It's how civilization has always worked, Princess. Latavia's problem is that you've become confused about this fundamental truth. You treat creatures as equals when they should serve as resources. You elevate the weak instead of celebrating the strong. It makes you... vulnerable."

"Or it makes us adaptable," Kira countered. "Strength comes in many forms, Your Highness. Sometimes the strongest choice is choosing mercy over cruelty."

"Mercy," Prince William repeated, as if tasting an unfamiliar word. "How... quaint. Well, you'll have plenty of opportunity to observe how Romalander strength manifests during your stay. Who knows? Perhaps you'll come to appreciate our perspective."

He stopped before an ornate door. "Here we are – your quarters, Princess. Sir Henry's room connects through there. I do hope you'll find everything satisfactory." Kira noticed a slight smirk on the prince's face.

Prince William pushed open the door to reveal a suite that was indeed satisfactory – luxurious, even. Rich fabrics, comfortable furniture, windows that overlooked gardens that were as geometrically perfect as everything else in this kingdom. It was also, Kira noticed immediately, designed more like a cage than a guest room. The windows had bars worked into their decorative ironwork. The door had locks on the outside as well as inside. The room could be sealed shut, trapping anyone inside.

"Beautiful," Kira managed. "Thank you, Your Highness."

"Rest now," Prince William said. "This evening, I'm hosting a small dinner in your honor. Nothing too elaborate – just an opportunity for you to meet some of our court's most influential members. I think you'll find the conversations... enlightening. And the menu quite exceptional. I've instructed my chef to prepare some of our finest traditional dishes. I do hope you'll be adventurous enough to try them."

The threat was clear. They would be served food that might well contain sentient beings, and refusing would be a diplomatic insult. Prince William was testing them, seeing how far they could be pushed, how much they would tolerate in the name of diplomacy.

"I look forward to it," Kira lied.

Prince William bowed, a gesture that managed to be both correct and mocking. "Until this evening, then." He departed, leaving them alone in rooms that felt more like a velvet-lined prison than guest quarters.

The moment the door closed, Kira crossed to the windows and tested the bars. Decorative they might be, but they were also solid iron, firmly anchored. Henry was already examining the walls, checking for listening holes or spy windows.

"We're trapped," Kira said quietly.

"We're exactly where we expected to be," Henry corrected, though his face was grim. "Prince William was never subtle about his intentions. At least now we know for certain that this is a trap."

Freddy the frog sat by the window.

"Freddy! If anyone finds you..."

"Then I'll be soup, I know," Freddy interrupted.

Henry crouched down to Freddy's level. "That's incredibly brave and incredibly foolish."

"I'm a frog, I need some sun, else I'll mold," Freddy replied. "Plus, brave and foolish is pretty much our entire personality." He hopped down, then toward the door, examining the gap beneath it. "Good. I can fit under there. I'll explore the castle tonight while you're at dinner, see what I can learn. Maybe find where they're keeping the creatures from that market, or where Prince William keeps his military plans."

"Freddy... make sure you're not on the menu," Kira started.

"Don't try to talk me out of it," the frog interrupted. "Might as well make myself useful. Just... try not to eat anything too horrifying at dinner, okay? I'd hate you to lose your nerve before we even get to the dangerous part of this mission."

Despite everything, Kira almost laughed. They were trapped in a hostile castle, surrounded by people who viewed thinking creatures as delicacies, about to attend a dinner where they'd be served who-knows-what while being evaluated as potential prisoners or worse. And their most reliable source of intelligence was a small green frog with suicidal courage and a talent for sarcasm.

"This is insane," she said.

"Completely," Henry agreed. "But we're committed now. We gather information, we document everything, we stay alive long enough to get that information back to your father, and we try very hard not to start a war in the process."

"Is that all?" Kira asked dryly.

"Well," Henry said with a slight smile, "we should also try not to get eaten. I feel like that should be on the list of priorities."

A knock on the door made them all freeze. Freddy disappeared under the bed in a blur of green. Henry moved to stand beside Kira as she called out, "Enter."

A servant opened the door, her face carefully blank. "Begging your pardon, Princess, but Prince William has sent refreshments for your comfort. And a message — he looks forward to introducing you to some very special guests at dinner tonight. Creatures you'll find quite fascinating, he says."

The servant set down a tray of food and drink, curtsied, and departed before Kira could respond. Henry immediately examined the tray, sniffing carefully at each item.

"Looks safe," he said. "Standard travel provisions — bread, cheese, preserved fruit. Nothing that screams 'drugged' or 'poisoned.'"

"But the message," Kira said. "Special guests. Creatures we'll find fascinating. Henry, what if—"

"What if he's captured more thinking beings for display?" Henry finished. "Or worse, for dinner? Then we'll witness it, document it, and use it as evidence when we return home." He looked at her seriously. "Kira, we have to be prepared to see terrible things tonight. Things we can't stop, can't prevent, can't even openly object to. Can you do that? Can you sit through a dinner where you might be watching creatures die and pretend to be a gracious, diplomatic guest?"

Kira thought about that fairy in the cage. About the creatures mounted on Prince William's walls. About Arnold's warning that she was walking into a trap specifically designed for her. She thought about her father's faith in her, about Latavia's need for intelligence, about all the lives that might depend on her keeping her composure no matter what horrors she witnessed.

"I don't know," she admitted. "But I'm going to try."

From under the bed, Freddy's voice emerged: "That's all anyone can do, Princess. Try. And if you fail, well... at least you'll have excellent company in the soup pot."

Despite everything, despite the fear and dread and overwhelming certainty that this was all going to end badly, Kira smiled. She had Henry, she had a brave if slightly unhinged frog, and she had her mother's blood running through her veins – blood that had survived secrets and dangers for years before Kira was born.

She could survive one dinner. Probably. She hoped. She'd better, because the alternative was too terrible to contemplate.

♠

The hours until dinner passed too quickly. Kira tried to rest, but her mind wouldn't quiet. Every creak of floorboards in the hall outside made her tense. Every distant shout or clash of metal from the training yards reminded her how thoroughly outnumbered they were. This castle probably housed a thousand soldiers. She had six guards, locked away in the outer barracks where they couldn't help her.

Henry spent the time reviewing Nesta's intelligence documents, committing names and faces to memory. "If we're going to meet influential court members tonight," he explained, "we should at least know who they are and what they control. Knowledge is armor when you don't have actual weapons."

Freddy, meanwhile, had taken it upon himself to explore every inch of the guest quarters, finding exits and hiding places, testing which floorboards creaked and which walls might contain passages. "Old castles always have secret ways," he explained. "Built for servants, or escape routes, or spying on guests. If I can find them, we might have ways out when we need them."

As sunset approached, a team of servants arrived to help Kira prepare for dinner. They brought jewelry, perfumes, everything needed to transform her from a travel-worn princess into a glittering example of Latavian royalty. Kira submitted to their ministrations while watching them carefully. Were they spies? Probably. Every servant in this castle likely reported back to Prince William.

The gown she chose for tonight was beautiful – deep crimson with gold embroidery that caught the light. It was also deliberately designed by the royal seamstress to restrict wing movement. The sleeves were tight, the skirt heavy and layered. If she needed to run or fight, she'd be severely hampered. After the servants finally left, Kira put on the gown and examined herself in the mirror, barely recognizing the person staring back. She looked like royalty, but she also looked like prey.

"You look beautiful," Henry said from the doorway. He'd been similarly transformed – formal Latavian court attire that made him look older, more serious, more like a diplomat and less like the warrior she knew. "And terrified."

"I am terrified," Kira admitted. "Henry, what if I can't do this? What if I see something that breaks me, and I lose control, and—"

He crossed to her, taking both her hands. "Then I'll pull you back. That's what I'm here for, Kira. To watch your back, to steady you when you falter, to remind you why we're here. We're not here to save everyone tonight. We're here to survive tonight so we can save everyone eventually."

A knock at the door announced the arrival of their escort – a cold-faced noble who introduced himself as Lord Ashton, one of Prince William's senior advisors. He led them through a maze of corridors, each more elaborate than the last, until they reached massive doors carved with scenes of Romalander history.

"The feast hall," Lord Ashton announced. "Prince William awaits."

Chapter 5 - The Prince's Castle

The feast hall was a monument to excess and a testament to cruelty disguised as sophistication. Crystal chandeliers cast warm light over tables that groaned under silver platters and golden goblets. Tapestries depicting Romalander victories covered the walls, but Kira's eyes were drawn to the centerpiece of the room – a massive display case, illuminated from within, showcasing what Prince William clearly considered his most prized possessions.

Creatures. Dozens of them. Each perfectly preserved in poses that suggested life – wings spread in flight, mouths open in silent calls, eyes that seemed to follow movement despite their glassy stillness. And beneath each one, a small plaque describing the species, when it was captured, and what made it special enough to warrant this eternal imprisonment.

"Magnificent, isn't it?" Prince William appeared at her elbow so silently that Kira jumped. His smile suggested he'd done it deliberately. "I call it my Gallery of Conquered Majesty. Each specimen represents something unique that I refused to let disappear from the world. That one there," he pointed to a creature with iridescent wings, "was a moon-singer. They're extinct now, but I managed to capture three before the species died out. Listen closely on certain nights, and you can still hear their songs echoing through the castle. At least, some of my servants claim they can. I think it's their imagination, but it adds a certain atmospheric quality to the halls, don't you think?"

Kira couldn't speak. The moon-singer's wings were spread in what might have been a defensive posture. Had it been trying to protect its nest when it was taken? Its young? The plaque didn't say.

"Princess Kira has always been fascinated by unique creatures," Henry said smoothly, saving her from having to respond. "In Latavia, we believe all life has value."

"How wonderfully egalitarian," Prince William replied. "But surely even Latavia recognizes that some life has more value than others? A human life versus a mouse, for instance. Or a noble bloodline versus common stock." His eyes flickered to Henry. "Or those born to rule versus those born to serve."

"We believe," Henry said carefully, "that value comes from choices and actions, not from birth."

"Choices," Prince William repeated, his tone making it clear what he thought of that philosophy. "Well, you'll have plenty of choices to make tonight. Choose wisely." He clapped his hands, and servants immediately began guiding guests to their seats.

The table arrangement was clearly calculated. Kira and Henry were separated, seated at different parts of the high table with Romalander nobles between them. Kira found herself wedged between Lord Ashton, who smelled of expensive wine and contempt, and a duchess whose name she didn't catch but whose jewelry featured what appeared to be actual preserved fairies.

As other guests arrived, Kira tried to aze them using Nesta's intelligence. Lord Hawkcroft, the military commander – scarred, serious, watching everything like a general assessing a battlefield. He was not only considered the 2nd most powerful man in Romaland after King Stephen, but also the king's childhood friend. The Lord's support from the generals and troops was legendary, and some thought his strategic mind had won Romaland's last three campaigns.

Lady Pemberton, who controlled the southern trade routes and wore her wealth like armor. Lord Blackwood, whose family had made their fortune in the exotic creature trade in South Romaland, causing many in that kingdom to have a price on *his* head. And a dozen others, each representing some aspect of North Romalander power and each looking at her like she was a puzzle to be solved or a threat to be neutralized.

Prince William stood at the head of the table, raising his golden goblet. "Friends, advisors, honored guests – welcome! Tonight, we celebrate the beginning of what I hope will be a lasting understanding between Romaland and Latavia. Princess Kira and Sir Henry have journeyed far to join us, demonstrating admirable courage in venturing into lands so different from their own. Let us show them the finest of Romalander hospitality!"

A cheer went up from the assembled nobles. Servants began bringing out the first course, and Kira's stomach clenched. The plates held what looked like small game birds, roasted and garnished. Normal enough, except—

"Quail," the duchess beside her explained. "Though not ordinary quail. These are from the southern forests, the variety that some claim can speak. Nonsense, of course. But they do have unusually large skulls for their size, which makes them quite flavorful. The brains, especially."

Kira stared at the bird on her plate. It looked ordinary. It might be ordinary. But the duchess had said "some claim can speak," and that horrible uncertainty was the point. Prince William wanted her to agonize over every bite, to wonder if she was consuming something that had thoughts and feelings.

She looked across the table and found Henry's eyes. He gave the slightest shake of his head. Don't refuse. Don't insult them. We have to play this through.

Kira picked up her fork. The quail might just be a bird. Or it might be murder disguised as dinner. She'd never know. And that was the most insidious torture of all.

Kira noticed Lord Hawkcroft, the military commander, wasn't eating either. He pushed the quail around his plate with the practiced movements of someone pretending to dine. When their eyes met briefly, she saw something unexpected; discomfort, perhaps even doubt. He looked away quickly, but not before she filed away that observation. Not everyone here was comfortable with Prince William's methods.

As she forced herself to eat, Lord Ashton engaged her in conversation. "Tell me, Princess, what do you think of our castle? I understand your castle is much smaller, less... organized."

"Different," Kira replied, choosing her words carefully. "We prioritize defense and functionality. This castle seems designed more for an impression."

"Everything Prince William does is designed for impression," Lord Ashton said with approval. "Wait until you see the ballroom he is building! Our prince understands that power is as much about perception as reality. Show strength, and others assume you have strength. Display dominance, and others accept your dominance. It's why his collection is so important – it demonstrates what happens to those who don't recognize their proper place in the natural order."

"And what is the natural order?" Kira asked, genuinely curious what answer he'd give.

"Humans at the top, as stewards of civilization," Lord Ashton replied as if it were obvious. "Among humans, those with strength, intelligence, and proper breeding rule. Those without serve. As for non-humans..." He gestured vaguely. "They exist for our use. Labor, food, entertainment, decoration. Some are more useful than others, but none are equal to humanity. To claim otherwise is to invite chaos."

"What about intelligent non-humans?" Kira pressed. "Creatures that can speak, reason, create?"

Lord Ashton's expression hardened. "Intelligence in an animal is like a parrot mimicking speech – interesting but ultimately meaningless. True intelligence requires not just cognition but proper form. A thinking beast is still a beast, Princess. Denying this truth doesn't change it. It just makes you vulnerable to manipulation by creatures that should be controlled."

The second course arrived, and this time there was no ambiguity. The servers placed elaborate platters in the center of the table, each holding a roasted creature that was clearly not ordinary livestock. One platter held something with visible scales and small horns. Another featured a bird with plumage that shimmered even in death. A third displayed what might have been a small primate, posed as if sleeping.

Prince William stood again, his smile radiant. "I'm particularly proud of tonight's main courses. Each represents a species we've recently brought to heel. The scaled drake from the eastern mountains – caught after a three-month hunt. The rainbow crow from the southern wetlands – the last of its kind, I'm told. And this," he indicated the primate-like creature, "is what the locals call a forest sage. They claim it could predict weather and find lost items. Imagine! Of course, it couldn't predict being found by my hunters." His audience laughed appreciatively.

Kira's hands clenched in her lap, hidden beneath the table's edge. She wanted to flip the table, draw her sword, challenge every person in this room to combat for their casual cruelty. She wanted to scream that these were beings, not food, that intelligence and consciousness should matter more than species.

But she couldn't. Because starting a fight here would mean death for her and Henry, failure of their mission, and likely war for Latavia. So instead, she took a carefully controlled breath and reached for her wine goblet, buying time to compose her face into something resembling calm interest.

"You seem disturbed, Princess," Prince William called down the table. "I hope you're not one of those who believes creatures are deserving of the same considerations as humans. That way lies madness and the collapse of civilization."

All eyes turned to her. This was a test, another in the series of tests Prince William had been conducting since they arrived. How would she respond? Would she defend Latavian values and mark herself as an enemy? Or would she bend, compromise, show weakness?

"I believe," Kira said slowly, choosing each word with extreme care, "that a wise ruler knows when to show mercy. And that true civilization is measured not by how we treat the strong, but by how we treat the vulnerable."

The table went silent. Prince William's expression was unreadable. Then he laughed, a sound that held no warmth. "How very Latavian. Tell me, Princess – when your kingdom falls to invasion, when your people are conquered and your lands occupied, will you comfort yourself with thoughts of how merciful you were? Will your vulnerability be worth the price?"

"We've held our borders for three centuries," Kira replied, her voice steady despite her racing heart. "And we've done it without sacrificing our humanity in the process."

"Humanity," Prince William mused. "Another interesting concept. What makes one human, I wonder? The shape of the body? The capacity for thought? Or is it something more... essential?" His gaze fixed on her with predatory intensity. "Some would argue that those with non-human traits, no matter how well hidden, can never truly be human. That mixing bloodlines creates something neither one thing nor another. Something unnatural that threatens the purity of both species."

The threat was barely veiled now. He was circling closer to her secret, testing to see if she'd react, if she'd give herself away.

"I would argue," Henry interjected, his voice carrying across the table, "that humanity is defined by our choices. By whether we choose cruelty or compassion, domination or cooperation. By that measure, some who look human might be monsters, while some who look monstrous might be the most human of us all."

"The orphaned Romalander speaks," Prince William said, his attention shifting. "Tell me, Sir Henry – do you ever wonder about your origins? About the family you lost when Latavia's soldiers raided that camp? I've been reviewing our records, and I believe I may have information about your bloodline. Wouldn't you like to know who you really are?"

Kira saw Henry's jaw tighten. This was another trap, dangling something precious – his identity, his history – as bait.

"I know who I am," Henry said firmly. "I'm a knight of Latavia, sworn to protect its people and uphold its values. My past doesn't change that."

"Doesn't it?" Prince William leaned back in his chair, clearly enjoying himself. "Bloodlines matter, Sir Henry. They determine so much – our strengths, our weaknesses, our fundamental nature. Learning your true heritage might explain things about yourself you've never understood. Might give you a sense of belonging you've been missing." He paused. "Or it might reveal that you're betraying your own people by serving Latavia."

"I'm not betraying anyone," Henry said, but Kira heard the uncertainty in his voice. Prince William had found his weakness – the gnawing need to know where he came from, who his people were.

"We'll discuss it more later," Prince William said dismissively. "For now, let's enjoy the feast! I've saved the best for last." He clapped his hands, and servants brought out a final covered platter, placing it directly in front of Kira. "Princess, would you do us the honor?"

Kira stared at the silver cover. Beneath it lay either ordinary food or another horror. Either way, she was expected to reveal it, to participate in whatever display Prince William had orchestrated.

She reached for the cover's handle. Her hand trembled slightly, and she forced it steady. Whatever was under there, she wouldn't give him the satisfaction of seeing her flinch.

She lifted the cover.

For a moment, she couldn't process what she was seeing. It was a cake, elaborately decorated with spun sugar and edible flowers. Beautiful. Harmless. Just a dessert.

Then she looked closer at the decorations. The flowers weren't made of sugar. They were real, preserved in honey, tiny and delicate. And they had faces. Miniature faces with expressions frozen in surprise or fear. Flower sprites, captured and crystallized in sweetness, now meant to be consumed as decoration.

"The northern flower sprites," Prince William explained to the fascinated nobles. "They live in the petals of certain rare blooms. Catching them requires remarkable patience and skill. My chef has preserved them in honey to maintain their delicate beauty. Each one adds a subtle floral note to the cake. Quite exquisite, really."

Kira's hands shook as she set down the cover. Those tiny faces stared up at her, preserved in amber sweetness like insects trapped in tree sap. Beings who had lived and thought and felt, reduced to garnish on a dessert meant to impress dinner guests.

"Princess?" Prince William's voice carried false concern. "You look pale. Perhaps the rich food has disagreed with you?"

This was it. The final test. Would she eat cake decorated with preserved sentient beings? Would she refuse and insult her host, giving him excuse to take offense? Or would she find some third option that might let her keep both her dignity and her dinner alliance intact?

"It's beautiful," Kira said, her voice surprisingly steady. "Too beautiful to eat, in fact. Such artistry should be preserved, not consumed. Might it be kept on display instead? I would hate to destroy such remarkable work."

Prince William's eyes narrowed slightly. She'd dodged his trap – admiring the creation without agreeing to eat it, showing appreciation without participating in the cruelty.

"How thoughtful," he said after a pause. "Though I assure you, my chef can create such works regularly. That's rather the point of using these creatures – they're plentiful enough to harvest but rare enough to impress." He gestured, and a servant began cutting the cake. "I insist you at least try a piece. It would offend my chef terribly if you refused to taste his masterwork."

The servant placed a slice before her, carefully positioned so that several of the preserved sprites decorated the top. Kira stared at it, her mind racing. She could refuse again, but that would escalate the confrontation. She could eat around the sprites, but that would be obvious and arguably more insulting. Or she could do what Henry had been trying to tell her all evening – make the terrible choice to survive long enough to stop this horror permanently.

She picked up her fork. Her hand moved as if independent from her mind, cutting a small piece from the edge of the cake, carefully avoiding the crystallized sprites. She brought the plain cake to her mouth, and in that moment, she understood something about her mother she'd never grasped before. This was what it meant to sacrifice yourself for your people – not dying gloriously in battle but walking the knife's edge between principle and survival. The cake tasted like ashes and honey, but at least she hadn't consumed the sprites.

"The cake itself is delicious," she said carefully, continuing to cut only from the undecorated portions. "Your chef is quite skilled." Prince William's eyes narrowed as he watched her surgical precision in avoiding the preserved sprites.

"You seem to be missing the most important garnishes, Princess."

"I find the cake sweet enough without them," Kira replied, meeting his gaze steadily. "Sometimes less is more." A flash of irritation crossed his face; she had technically tasted his "masterwork" while avoiding the true horror of it. She'd found a middle path he hadn't anticipated.

"You know, Princess Kira, you're far craftier than I expected. When I first heard about Latavia's peculiar values, I thought you'd be weak, easily broken by exposure to proper civilization. But you're proving surprisingly resilient. Perhaps there's hope for diplomatic understanding between our kingdoms after all."

"Understanding requires both parties to listen," Kira managed.

"Indeed," Prince William agreed. "And I've been listening very carefully. Learning all sorts of fascinating things about you and your kingdom." He stood, raising his goblet once more. "A toast! To new alliances, to understanding between peoples, and to the natural order that allows the strong to guide the weak toward their proper place in the world!"

The nobles drank. Kira raised her goblet but barely let the wine touch her lips. Across the table, Henry's face was carefully blank, but she could read the pain in his eyes. He'd watched her compromise, watched her eat that cake, and he understood what it cost her.

After dinner, Prince William announced his intention to give them a complete tour of the castle. "You should see all that Romaland has accomplished," he explained. "All that we've built through strength and proper order."

The tour was another exercise in horror disguised as hospitality. Each room revealed new evidence of Romaland's systematic cruelty. A library whose shelves held not just books but preserved specimens used as decorative bookends. A trophy room where mounted creatures covered every wall, their plaques describing how they were hunted, captured, and killed. A gallery of portraits showing Romalander nobles posing with their most prized catches, many of which were clearly sentient beings treated like game animals.

But the worst was saved for last. Prince William led them to a door at the base of one of the towers, his expression almost gleeful. "This is my favorite part of the castle. My personal collection, separate from the public displays. These specimens are too valuable, too rare, to risk damage from casual viewing."

He unlocked the door and led them down a spiral staircase into cool darkness. Torches flickered to life as they descended, revealing a vast underground chamber. And everywhere Kira looked, she saw cages.

Dozens of them. Hundreds of them. Each containing a creature that was clearly more than just an animal. They lined the walls, stacked in careful rows, each with a small plaque describing its occupant. And unlike the preserved specimens upstairs, these creatures were alive.

A small dragon curled in one cage, its scales dull with captivity. It had a leather muzzle over its mouth and a steel plate blocking its nostrils. It could barely breathe in air, let alone unleash fire. Without airflow, the dragon was powerless; fire required breath, and Prince William had made certain the creature could barely draw enough air to survive.

In another, something that looked like a miniature person with butterfly wings pressed against the bars, eyes hopeless. A cage near the entrance held what appeared to be a young troll, separated from its twin, whimpering softly in the darkness.

"My breeding stock," Prince William explained proudly. "And my insurance policy. Each of these creatures represents a species or bloodline I'm preserving. When they breed, I can harvest the young for feasts or trade. When they fail to breed, well..." He gestured to the stuffed specimens visible through an archway. "Nothing goes to waste."

Kira felt her composure cracking. This was beyond horror. This was systematic, planned, organized evil dressed up as conservation and culture.

"You breed them?" Henry's voice was hoarse. "You keep them in cages, force them to produce offspring, and then—"

"I ensure their species survive," Prince William corrected. "Left in the wild, most of these creatures would be extinct within a generation. Here, they're protected, fed, cared for. Yes, I use their offspring as I see fit, but that's the price of preservation. Everything has a cost, Sir Henry."

"Everything has a price," Kira said, her voice emerging stronger than she felt. "And someday, you'll pay for this."

Prince William turned to face her, and for the first time, his mask of civility slipped. His expression was cold, calculating, and absolutely certain of his power. "Are you threatening me, Princess? In my own castle, surrounded by my guards, having just eaten my food and accepted my hospitality?"

"I'm observing," Kira replied, meeting his gaze. "That this isn't civilization. It's cruelty with better decorations."

"And yet you ate the cake," Prince William said softly. "You compromised your precious Latavian values to avoid insulting me. You've already chosen survival over principles once tonight. How many more times will you compromise, I wonder, before you realize that your values are luxuries you can't afford?"

He was right, and Kira hated him for it. She had compromised. She'd eaten that cursed cake. She'd toured these horrors and bit her tongue rather than screaming her rage. She'd failed every test of character she'd faced, all in service of the mission, of gathering intelligence, of surviving to warn her father.

"I think," Henry said carefully, stepping between them, "that the princess is tired from the journey and the rich food. Perhaps we should retire for the evening? We can continue discussions tomorrow when everyone is better rested."

Prince William's gaze lingered on Kira for another heartbeat, then he smiled again. "Of course. How thoughtless of me, keeping you up so late after your travels. Lord Ashton will escort you back to your rooms." He turned to leave, then paused. "Oh, and Princess? Don't bother trying to free any of my collection. The cages are locked with keys only I possess, and the tower is guarded day and night. Even if you managed to open one cage, you'd never get the occupant out of the castle alive. Better to accept reality and focus on our treaty negotiations tomorrow."

He ascended the stairs, leaving them in the chamber of cages with Lord Ashton's cold presence at their backs. As they climbed back toward the castle proper, Kira heard sounds from the cages – whimpers, quiet sobs, the rustle of creatures too broken by captivity to even hope for rescue.

♠

Back in her guest room, with the door firmly locked from the outside, Kira pressed her hands against her face, shoulders shaking with silent fury and grief. A soft knock at the connecting door to Henry's room made her look up. He entered without waiting for permission, his own face showing the strain of the evening.

"Don't," he said before she could speak. "Don't apologize, don't beat yourself up, don't tell me you failed. You survived. That's what matters."

"I ate...

"You survived," Henry repeated firmly. "And you gathered intelligence. We now know that Prince William keeps breeding stock of endangered creatures. He's systematically hunting species to extinction while claiming to preserve them. That his castle has an entire underground prison full of beings we might be able to help if we can figure out how. That's valuable information, Kira. Worth the cost."

"Is it?" Kira whispered. "Worth eating something that might have had thoughts and dreams? Worth compromising who I am?"

"Yes," Henry said, though his voice cracked slightly. "Because if we'd refused, if we'd made a stand tonight, we'd be in cages ourselves by morning. Or dead. And no one would ever know what Prince William is really doing here. Your father needs this intelligence. Latavia needs it. And those creatures in those cages need someone who knows they exist and has the power to do something about it."

A rustling from beneath the bed announced Freddy's return. The frog emerged, looking shaken. "I found the kitchens. And the storage rooms. And places I really wish I'd never seen. But I also found something interesting." He hopped onto the table between them. "The gold feather symbol Arnold mentioned? It's carved into the bottom shelf of the third pantry in the east kitchen. And there are supplies hidden there – traveling cloaks, dried food, maps. Someone in this castle is part of the underground network."

"Someone here is helping creatures escape?" Henry asked.

"Planning to," Freddy confirmed. "There's also a drainage system that runs from those cage chambers out to the river beyond the castle walls. Big enough for small creatures to squeeze through. Maybe even big enough for a determined frog to explore." He looked at them seriously. "We can't free everyone. We don't have time, resources, or keys. But we might be able to help a few. Start building relationships with the underground. Plant seeds for future resistance."

Kira felt something spark in her chest – not quite hope, but close. Purpose. Direction. A way to take action instead of just surviving horrors.

"Tomorrow," she said, "Prince William wants to begin treaty negotiations. He'll try to trap me with words the same way he trapped me with that cake tonight. But while he's focused on breaking me in the negotiation room, you two can explore. Find that underground contact. Map those drainage tunnels. Figure out if there's any way to get messages to Latavia without the Romalanders intercepting them."

"And what will you do?" Henry asked.

Kira's expression hardened. "I'll negotiate. I'll smile and bow and pretend to consider his terms. And I'll make him so confident that he's won, so certain that I'm broken and compromised, that he doesn't notice us gathering everything we need to destroy him."

"That's a dangerous game," Henry warned.

"Everything about this is dangerous," Kira replied. "But I'd rather play dangerous games than sit passive while creatures suffer. My mother hid her nature for years to protect me and Latavia. I can pretend to compromise for a few days to protect everyone else."

Freddy hopped up on the windowsill, peering out at the moonlit castle grounds. "The question is – how long can we keep up the act before Prince William decides the game is over and springs whatever final trap he's been planning?"

"I can't sleep," Kira said as she struggled to get out of the gown as she ducked behind a screen. "Get changed," she commanded. "We're going exploring."

Chapter 6 - Underground Networks

The servant's corridor was darker than the dungeons, if such a thing were possible. Kira pressed herself against the damp stone wall, listening to Henry's breathing beside her. They'd been searching for Nesta's resistance contact for three hours, following cryptic directions whispered by a kitchen maid with frightened eyes.

"This is insane," Henry whispered, his breath warm against her ear. "We should go back before..."

A blade pressed against his throat, cutting off his words.

"Before someone finds you?" A woman's voice, amused and dangerous. "Too late for that, Latavian."

Kira's hand moved to her concealed dagger, but the woman laughed. "Princess Kira. Sir Henry. Relax. If I wanted you dead, you'd never have heard me coming."

The blade withdrew. In the dim light filtering through a grate above, Kira could make out sharp features and intelligent eyes. Elena, leader of Romaland's underground resistance. Just how Nesta had described her.

"You're either very brave or very stupid, seeking us out," Elena said, gesturing for them to follow. "Prince William has been particularly... creative with captured resistance members lately."

They descended through a hidden panel into tunnels that ran beneath the castle proper. The air grew warmer, tinged with unfamiliar scents—herbs, smoke, and something wild that made Kira's transformation instincts stir.

"Control it," Elena said sharply, noticing Kira's slight tremor. "We have traps down here for raptors' wings," Elena said as she pointed to the rafters. "They are called silk-snakes and are deadly. Brush against them and you'll be snagged in their nets, covered in threads, and then paralyzed."

"You know what I am?" Kira asked.

"I know you're not the only one." Elena pushed open a heavy door, revealing a vast underground chamber. "Welcome to the real Romaland."

The room was filled with beings of every description; some fully human, others bearing obvious magical heritage, and many somewhere in between. Children with scales played alongside elderly women whose eyes held ancient wisdom. A man with partial wing structures taught a group to read by candlelight. Kira noticed Elena's eyes tracking the preserved specimens with a mixture of reverence and grief.

"My God," Henry breathed. "How many?"

"Hundreds here. Thousands throughout the kingdom." Elena's expression hardened. "This is what Prince William's 'progress' looks like. Anyone with a drop of magical blood, anyone who shows signs of gifts, anyone who even sympathizes—they disappear. We catch who we can."

A small girl tugged at Kira's sleeve. She couldn't have been more than six, with silvery hair and eyes that shifted color like sunset clouds. "Are you here to save us?"

Kira knelt, her heart breaking. "What's your name?"

"Lily. My mama said someone would come. Someone who could fly."

Henry's hand found Kira's shoulder, squeezing gently. She felt the weight of his touch, the unspoken support. Looking up, she caught his expression—pride, worry, and something deeper she didn't dare name.

"We're going to try, Lily," Kira promised.

Elena scoffed. "Try? You're two diplomats playing games in a castle while we—"

An explosion rocked the chamber. Dust rained from the ceiling as screams erupted.

"Raid!" someone shouted. "They've found us!"

Romalander soldiers poured through multiple entrances, weapons raised. Not normal weapons—the silk-snakes nets and chains Kira had seen in the dungeons, designed to trap magical beings.

"Run!" Elena commanded, drawing twin blades. "Southern tunnels! Go!"

But there were too many soldiers, too few exits. Kira watched in horror as silk-snake nets descended on fleeing civilians. Lily stood frozen, tears streaming down her color-shifting eyes.

Henry moved without hesitation, scooping up the girl and two other children. "Kira, we need to..."

A net caught him mid-sentence, silk-snake threads wrapping around his legs. He went down hard, shielding the children with his body as soldiers advanced.

"Henry!"

Kira's decision wasn't conscious. One moment she was human, the next her wings exploded from her back, shredding her diplomatic dress. She launched herself across the chamber, talons extended, catching the nearest soldier across the chest. His armor shrieked as her claws found purchase.

"Raptor!" someone screamed. "The princess is a raptor!"

She didn't care. Henry was trapped, more nets flying toward him and the children. Kira dove, her wings creating a wind that sent soldiers stumbling. She grabbed the silk-snakes net with her talons, ignoring the burning pain as the cursed silk seared her skin. With a powerful beat of her wings, she tore it apart.

Henry looked up at her, and time seemed to stop. His eyes held wonder, not fear. "Kira..."

"Can you run?"

He nodded, gathering the children. But more soldiers were coming, and Kira could see Prince William's personal guard among them. They'd been set up.

"Everyone down!" Elena shouted.

The resistance leader threw something—a crystal that shattered against the floor. Light exploded through the chamber, blinding in its intensity. When it faded, half the soldiers were unconscious, the silk-snake's weapons somehow neutralized.

"Expensive trick," Elena panted. "Won't work twice. Move!"

They ran through twisting passages, Kira's wings folded but still visible, no point in hiding now. Henry stayed close, with one hand occasionally brushing her feathers as if to assure himself they were real.

"That was incredible," he said as they paused to catch their breath. "You were incredible."

"I blew our cover," Kira said miserably. "Prince William will..."

"You saved those children." Henry stepped closer, his hand cupping her face. "You saved me. We now know what we're up against. I've seen you fight, Kira, but this... seeing you fly, seeing you choose to reveal yourself to protect others..." His thumb traced her cheekbone. "How did I get lucky enough to know you?"

Before she could respond, Elena interrupted. "Touching moment, but we have bigger problems. That raid wasn't random. Someone knew exactly where to find us, exactly when you'd be here."

"A trap," Kira said, ice in her veins.

"Or a test." Elena's expression was grim. "Either way, Prince William knows what you are. The question is, what does he plan to do about it?"

Chapter 7 - The Test of Loyalty

Prince William was waiting in their quarters when they returned, seated casually in Henry's chair with a glass of wine. Owen stood behind him, face carefully neutral.

"Princess Kira," William said pleasantly. "You've had an eventful evening."

Kira's hand moved to her sword, but William merely smiled. "Please. If I wanted you arrested, you'd be in chains already. Sit. Both of you." He handed her a scroll. "We're here to sign a treaty, not start a war."

They remained standing, but Kira opened the scroll.

"I must confess," William continued, "I'm impressed. A raptor in Latavia's royal line. Your father hid it well. Though I suppose your mother's death makes more sense now."

Kira's breath caught. Her mother, Kirena, had died because she was a raptor?

"You're lying," Henry said firmly.

"I've studied raptors for years; they don't handle the plague well. Is it harder to keep your wings constrained when you're sick? What about during extreme emotional distress, perhaps? Fear? Anger?" William's eyes glinted. "Or love?"

His gaze shifted meaningfully to Henry, and Kira's stomach clenched.

"What do you want?" she asked.

"What I've always wanted. Progress. Evolution. Controlled, directed, useful evolution." William stood, moving to the window. "You think me a monster for how I treat magical creatures. But look at what uncontrolled magic does; chaos in the streets, bloodlines corrupted, traditional structures collapsed. I seek to harness that power, not destroy it. Find ways to cure them during a plague. I could have saved your mother. "

"By enslaving beings and treating them as property?"

"By creating order from chaos." William turned back to them. "Your little rescue mission tonight saved, what, thirty beings?

Forty? I have hundreds in my facilities. But here's the interesting part, I'm going to let you visit them. Officially. Tomorrow. Before you sign that treaty in your hands."

Henry stepped forward. "Why?"

"Because I want Princess Kira to understand what's at stake. And because..." William's smile was predatory, "I want her to sign that willingly. "

He moved toward the door, Owen following. "Rest well. Tomorrow will be educational and exciting."

As the door closed, Kira sank into a chair, reading the treaty. Henry immediately knelt beside her, taking her free hand.

"He's planning something," Henry said.

"Of course he is." Kira looked at their joined hands. "Henry, what he said about my mother..." The treaty fell to the floor.

"Changes nothing." His voice was fierce. "You are not responsible for how you were born, only for what you choose to do with your gifts. And what I saw tonight? You chose to save lives, even at the cost of your secret."

"I couldn't watch you die."

Henry's hands tightened on hers.

"Kira, I need to tell you something. When I saw you transform, when you flew across that chamber to save me, I realized—"

A knock interrupted. Owen entered, looking uncomfortable. "Your Highnesses. Prince William wanted me to inform you that tomorrow's tour will include a demonstration. He suggests you rest. And Princess..." He hesitated. "He said to tell you that raptors are particularly susceptible to silk-snakes poisoning. The burns on your talons should be treated immediately."

He left a medical kit and departed quickly.

Henry immediately examined Kira's hands, finding the angry burns where she'd grabbed the net. "These look painful."

"Worth it," she said softly.

As he carefully applied salve to her wounds, his touch infinitely gentle, Kira found herself studying his face. The concentration in his eyes, the worried crease in his brow, the way he cradled her hands like they were precious.

"What were you going to say?" she asked. "Before Owen interrupted?"

Henry looked up, meeting her eyes. "That I've been an idiot. I've been so focused on protecting you, on being the perfect knight, that I almost missed what's right in front of me."

"Which is?"

"That somewhere between fighting enchanted forests and navigating Romalander politics, I fell in love with you."

Kira's heart stopped. "Henry..."

"I know. I know we can't, I know your father would kill me, I know there are a thousand reasons why—"

She kissed him, cutting off his protests. It was desperate and sweet and tasted of possibilities they might never have. When they pulled apart, both were breathless.

"I love you too," she whispered. "I think I have for a while."

"Terrible timing," he said, though he was smiling.

"The worst."

They stayed close, foreheads touching, hands entwined.

"Whatever Prince William shows us tomorrow," Henry said, "whatever he offers—we face it together."

"Together," Kira agreed.

♠

In his tower, Prince William smiled as Owen delivered his report. The princess had revealed her gift to save the knight. The knight had declared his love. The new treaty was on the floor, ignored.

Perfect.

Love was just another weapon, after all. And Prince William had become quite skilled at turning weapons against their wielders.

"Double the silk-snakes in the demonstration hall," he ordered. "And ensure the special subjects are prepared. Tomorrow, we discover just how far Princess Kira will go for love."

Owen bowed, though his expression was troubled. "And if she refuses your offer?"

"Then we'll have two new specimens for the research division." William's smile widened. "A raptor princess and her devoted knight. Think of what we could learn."

As Owen departed to carry out his orders, Prince William returned to his maps. War was coming, whether through treaty or conquest. But now he had leverage—Kira's secret, her love for the knight, and most importantly, her desperate need to save everyone.

Heroes were so predictable. And that predictability would be her downfall.

Chapter 8 - The Feast of Horrors

Kira spent the full day studying the treaty that Prince William had handed her. Henry paced back and forth, asking questions.

"They want us to do what?"

"Clear out the forbidden lands of all non-humans," Kira replied. "Same with the enchanted forest, chop down all the mother trees."

"They want to harvest all the saplings, to make better weapons," Henry said as Kira got up and walked to the window.

"I can't sign this; my father will never sign it either." Henry joined her at the window. He handed her a piece of bread.

"Eat, rest," he said as he noticed the sun setting. "Owen sent a message that the signing celebration would start at sunset."

♠

Later, Kira stood in her chambers, staring at her reflection in the polished mirror. She'd dressed in the finest gown her servants had packed for her. It was a deep red silk that contrasted with her eyes, making her look every inch the royal princess. The gold feather pendant hung at her throat, visible to anyone who knew what to look for. Elena would see it. The network members would see it. They would know she was committed.

Under the elaborate gown, she'd strapped on thin leather armor and concealed two blades. If tonight went as badly as she expected, she'd need to fight her way out. And this time, she was done pretending to be just a diplomat.

Henry knocked and entered, similarly dressed in formal attire that concealed his own weapons. His face was set in grim determination. "Freddy made contact with Elena. The plan is set. During the feast, while Prince William is distracted, we slip away using the servants' passages. Elena will have guides waiting to lead the freed creatures to the drainage tunnels." The cook had told her later that she'd tried dozens of times to access Prince William's private study; once even getting as far as the tapestry, but guards rotated unpredictably and the risks had always been too great. Maybe a thinking creature as small and invisible as Freddy could accomplish what the resistance couldn't.

"How long do we have?" Kira asked.

"An hour, maybe less. Once Prince William notices we're missing, he'll send guards. We need to be in the tunnels with the last of the creatures before that happens." Henry paused. "Kira, there's still time to back out. We could sit through this feast, endure whatever horrors it contains, maintain our diplomatic cover..."

"And then what?" Kira interrupted. "Go home and tell my father that we negotiated with monsters and learned absolutely nothing useful except that they're worse than we imagined? That we watched thinking beings die and did nothing? That we had a chance to save some of them and chose safety instead?" She shook her head. "I can't do that, Henry. I can't be that person."

"I know," Henry said softly. "I just needed to hear you say it one more time. To be sure you'd made peace with what comes next."

"I haven't made peace with anything," Kira admitted. "But I've made my choice."

A sharp knock announced their escort's arrival. Lord Ashton stood in the corridor, his expression as cold and proper as ever. "Prince William requests your presence, Princess. The feast is about to begin."

They followed him through corridors that felt more like a death march than a walk to dinner. Kira's heart pounded against her ribs, her wings strained against the thick fabric of her gown. Each step was bringing her closer to whatever horror awaited in that great hall. She focused on breathing, on maintaining her composure, knowing that soon... very soon... she would finally take action instead of just enduring.

The great hall doors opened, and sound washed over them. Romalander nobles filled every seat, dressed in their finest, drinking freely, laughing with the careless cruelty of people who'd never questioned their right to do terrible things. Musicians played in the corner, their music almost managing to mask the underlying tension that Kira felt crackling through the air.

Prince William stood at the head table, resplendent in dark blue velvet trimmed with silver. He raised his goblet as Kira and Henry entered, and the hall quieted.

"Our guests of honor!" Prince William announced. "Princess Kira, whose remarkable skill provided tonight's main course. Sir Henry, whose Romalander blood runs true despite years of Latavian influence. Welcome! Please, take your places. Tonight we celebrate not just the hunt, but the progress of our treaty negotiations and the growing understanding between our kingdoms."

Kira let herself be guided to her seat, positioned – of course – directly facing the preparation table where the feast's centerpiece would soon be displayed. The placement was deliberate, ensuring she couldn't look away, couldn't pretend not to see whatever horror Prince William had orchestrated.

The first courses arrived quickly – soups, breads, roasted vegetables. Normal food, carefully designed to lull guests into thinking this might be a standard feast. Kira picked at her plate, not trusting anything served in this hall, waiting for the inevitable moment when normalcy gave way to nightmare.

Prince William stood again, this time holding a scroll. "Before we proceed to the main course, I thought we might discuss the treaty terms. Princess Kira, have you had time to review my new treaty? Do you come bearing Latavia's response?"

This was it. The moment she'd been dreading and preparing for. Kira stood, pulling out her own document – the carefully worded response she and Henry had drafted, full of diplomatic language that said essentially nothing while sounding significant.

"Your Highness," she began, her voice carrying across the suddenly quiet hall. "I've reviewed your treaty with care. While Latavia appreciates Romaland's interest in formal alliance, we have concerns about several provisions... the enchanted forest, the forbidden lands."

Henry spoke up, "and your classification system of all our citizens... this would..."

"Concerns," Prince William interrupted, his smile sharp. "How diplomatic. Tell me, Princess, are your concerns philosophical or practical? Do you object to the principle, or merely the details of its implementation?"

Kira took a breath, choosing her next words with extreme care. This was her last chance to maintain diplomatic cover, to keep the door open for peaceful resolution. Once she spoke her true mind, there would be no going back.

She thought about those young trolls, probably being prepared in the kitchens right now. About the creatures in the breeding cages who'd been waiting for years for someone to care enough to help them. About her mother's hidden wings and her father's desperate hope for peace. About Peek and Aboo, who had saved her life and whose kindred were treated as delicacies in this kingdom. About people like Henry, made into slaves.

"I object to the principle," she said clearly. "The classification system you propose treats thinking beings as resources to be managed rather than individuals with rights. Latavia cannot and will not participate in any system that categorizes sentient creatures as property based on their species or heritage."

The hall went absolutely silent. Prince William's expression didn't change, but something cold flickered in his eyes. "I see. And you speak for King Phillip in this rejection?"

"I speak for myself," Kira replied. "But I believe my father will agree when I report what I've witnessed here. The markets where intelligent creatures are sold like livestock. The breeding chambers where beings are imprisoned to produce offspring for feasts. The hunts where thinking creatures are killed for sport. This isn't civilization, Your Highness. It is systematic cruelty dressed up with fancy words."

Lord Ashton surged to his feet, his face flushed with wine and anger. "You dare insult Romalander culture while accepting our hospitality? While sitting in our hall, eating our food..."

"I haven't eaten your food," Kira interrupted. "Not willingly. Not the parts that matter. And I'm done pretending to accept hospitality that comes at the price of beings' lives and dignity."

Prince William raised a hand, silencing Lord Aston. His gaze fixed on Kira with predatory intensity. "Strong words, Princess. I wonder if you'll maintain such conviction when you see what your 'remarkable skill' in yesterday's daring escape has provided for tonight's feast."

He gestured, and servants began wheeling in the main course. Kira had been bracing herself for horror, but nothing could have fully prepared her for what she saw.

The young twin trolls – or what had been the darling young trolls – had been roasted and arranged on massive silver platters, displayed as if they were simply oversized game animals. Garnishes surrounded them, making the presentation almost artistic in its monstrous precision. And positioned on the table nearest Kira was something worse – small silver cards describing each troll, their approximate age, where they'd been captured, and suggested cooking times for anyone who wanted to try the recipe at home.

Kira's vision went red at the edges. She heard a roaring in her ears that might have been her own blood or might have been something deeper, older, more primal. Her raptor heritage, kept carefully hidden for years, tugged against the gown that bound her wings.

"You monster," she whispered.

"I'm a realist," Prince William corrected. "And a reminder, Princess – you put the arrow in that tree. You marked them for the hunt. Your skill, as I announced to the hall, provided this feast. So, when you call me a monster, remember that you participated. You compromised. You chose survival over principle when it mattered."

He was right, and that made it worse. Kira had tried to save them and failed, but in trying she'd marked them as her quarry, made herself complicit in their deaths. Prince William had maneuvered her into a position where even her attempted mercy had been turned into collaboration with cruelty.

"Princess Kira," Prince William continued, his voice carrying across the silent hall. "I offer you one final chance to demonstrate wisdom. Eat. Partake of the feast your warrior skills provided. Show Latavia's willingness to embrace practical reality over sentimental principle. Do this, and we can continue our negotiations in good faith. Refuse..." He paused meaningfully. "Well, refusal would be a grave insult to Romalander hospitality. It might even be considered an act of war."

Every eye in the hall was on her. The Romalander nobles watched with expressions ranging from anticipation to disgust – apparently even some of them found this test excessive. The servants stood frozen, uncertain. And Henry sat beside her, his hand moving slowly toward his concealed weapon, ready to fight if she gave the signal.

Kira looked at the platters. They had trusted her enough to play dead at her instruction. Who had never hurt anyone, who had just lived in their forest until Prince William's hunters had caged them for sport.

She thought about Peek and Aboo, who had chosen her friendship over hunger. Who had saved her life and earned their place at Castle Latavia's table through courage and loyalty. Who would be heartbroken to know their young kindred had died this way.

She thought about her mother, who had hidden her wings for years and made a thousand small compromises to protect what mattered. But who had also told Kira, in that last conversation before the plague took her, "A wise ruler knows when to hide and when to reveal. When to bend and when to break. Choose your moments carefully, my daughter, but when the moment comes – don't hesitate."

This was the moment.

Kira stood slowly, her chair scraping against stone in the silence. She looked directly at Prince William, her voice clear and unwavering.

"No."

The word hung in the air like a thrown gauntlet.

"I will not eat beings who trusted me. I will not participate in this horror you call civilization. And I will not negotiate any treaty that requires Latavia to adopt your monstrous philosophy." She pulled off the diplomatic mask she'd been wearing for days and let Prince William see the fury beneath. "You wanted to test me? To see if I could be broken, if I could be made to compromise my values? Congratulations. You've succeeded in showing me exactly what Romaland is – and what it will never be allowed to become in Latavia."

"You're declaring war," Prince William said softly, dangerously.

"You declared war when you caged thinking beings," Kira shot back. "When you hunted creatures for sport. When you tried to force me to participate in atrocities. I'm just finally acknowledging it." She pulled out the treaty document and tore it in half, letting the pieces fall to the floor. "There will be no alliance between our kingdoms. No trade agreements. No cooperation. Latavia will oppose everything Romaland represents, and we will do it knowing that we chose principle over safety."

"You're a fool," Prince William said, standing now as well. "And you've just condemned your kingdom to invasion and conquest. Latavia cannot stand against Romaland's combined armies. After South Romaland hears how you ate their kindred, they will join us in defeating Latavia. You know this."

"Maybe," Kira admitted. "But we'll stand anyway. Because some things are worth fighting for even when you know you'll lose. Honor. Compassion. The belief that intelligence and consciousness matter more than species or strength." She met his eyes. "And the absolute certainty that your way is wrong."

Prince William's facade of civility finally cracked completely. "Guards! Seize them both. Princess Kira and Sir Henry are hereby declared enemies of the newly united Romaland, to be held for trial and punishment for their crimes against our kingdoms."

Guards began moving toward the high table from all sides. Henry was on his feet instantly, drawing his sword. Kira drew her own concealed blades, backing toward Henry until they stood together, weapons raised, facing down two dozen armed soldiers in a hall full of hostile nobles.

"This is suicide," Henry muttered.

"Probably," Kira agreed. "But I'm tired of surviving at the cost of my soul. At least this way we go down fighting."

"For what it's worth," Henry said as the guards closed in, "I agree with every word you said. And I'm honored to stand with you."

"Even if it means dying in a foreign castle far from home?"

"Especially then," Henry replied. "Some company makes even death bearable."

The first guard reached them, sword raised. Henry parried the blow and countered with a strike that sent the man stumbling back. Kira engaged two more, her blades flashing in the torchlight. She was outnumbered, out positioned, and fighting in formal wear that restricted her movement. But she was also furious, righteously so, and that fury gave her strength.

For a few glorious moments, they held the guards back. Henry fought with the skill of someone who'd trained since childhood, every move precise and efficient. Kira fought with the passion of someone who had finally stopped compromising, who had chosen her stand and would defend it to her last breath.

But skill and passion could only do so much against overwhelming numbers. A guard's club caught Henry across the shoulders, sending him to his knees. Another grabbed Kira's arm, twisting until she dropped one blade. She kicked him away and spun to help Henry, but three more guards tackled her from behind, bearing her to the ground under their weight.

"Enough!" Prince William's voice cut through the chaos. "Take them alive. I want them conscious for what comes next."

Rough hands hauled Kira to her feet, wrenching her arms behind her back. Across the hall, Henry was similarly restrained, blood trickling from a cut on his forehead. They'd fought well, but it had never been a fight they could win.

Prince William descended from the high table, approaching Kira with measured steps. His expression was no longer amused or condescending. Now it was simply cold, calculating, and absolutely certain of his power.

"You could have had peace," he said quietly, for her ears alone. "You could have signed the treaty, maintained the diplomatic fiction, given your father time to prepare for inevitable conflict. Instead, you chose to make a scene. To declare opposition publicly. To force my hand." He studied her face. "I wonder – was it worth it? This moment of moral superiority? Because it will cost you everything."

"Yes," Kira said without hesitation. "It was worth it. Because for the first time in days, I'm not ashamed of my choices."

Something flickered in Prince William's expression – not respect, exactly, but perhaps recognition. "You're your mother's daughter," he said. "My father knew Queen Kirena, before her death. He knew what she was. What you are." His hand moved to her throat, fingers closing around the gold feather pendant. "And I know what this means. The underground network you've been conspiring with. The escape plan for my breeding stock."

He yanked the pendant free, the chain breaking. Kira's heart sank. He'd known. All along, he'd known what she was planning.

"Did you really think you could free my collection without me noticing?" Prince William asked, loud enough now for the hall to hear. "That I wouldn't have spies in Elena's pathetic resistance network? I've known about tonight's plan since before you arrived at my castle. The whole thing was a trap, Princess. Just like everything else."

He gestured, and guards dragged a struggling figure into the hall. Elena's face was bruised, her hands bound, but her eyes were defiant.

"Your underground contact," Prince William announced. "Arrested an hour ago along with a dozen other conspirators. Their escape tunnels are sealed. Their safe houses raided. And any creatures they thought they'd saved..." He smiled cruelly. "Well, they're being returned to my collection even as we speak. You didn't save anyone, Princess. You just exposed the one network that was actually helping creatures escape."

The words hit Kira like physical blows. Elena. The network. The creatures they'd hoped to save. All of it compromised, destroyed, because she'd been arrogant enough to think she could outsmart Prince William on his own ground.

"Take them to the breeding chambers," Prince William ordered. "Put Princess Kira in the raptor cage – I've been keeping it empty specifically for her. Sir Henry can go in with the human prisoners. And Elena..." He considered. "She can watch what happens to those who betray Romalander hospitality. Chain her where she has a good view."

As guards began dragging them away, Prince William called out one last time. "Oh, and Princess? I'll be sending Lord Marcus to Latavia in the morning with a declaration of war and evidence of your crimes. Your father will learn that his daughter conspired with traitors, rejected legitimate treaty offers, and assaulted Romalander nobles in their own hall. He'll have a choice – disavow you and possibly salvage peace, or defend you and guarantee invasion." He paused. "I wonder which he'll choose? Family or kingdom? Love or duty? It will be interesting to see if Latavian values hold up when the cost becomes real."

Kira wanted to spit back defiance, to tell him that her father would never abandon her, that Latavia would fight.

"'Lord Marcus travels with a full delegation and slower cavalry,' Prince William continued. 'Four days for him to reach Latavia and return. That's when this becomes real. That's when your father makes his choice—sign the treaty I've already sent with him, or condemn his people to war. Use that time, Princess. Convince yourself it's worth it.'"

But she couldn't speak past the crushing weight of failure. She'd tried to save creatures and got the resistance network destroyed. She'd tried to stand on principle and gotten herself and Henry captured. She'd thought she was being brave when she was actually being reckless.

And now everyone would pay the price for her choices.

♠

The breeding chambers beneath the tower were darker than Kira remembered, lit only by a few sputtering torches that cast more shadows than light. The guards who'd dragged her down the spiral stairs were efficient and impersonal, following orders without comment or cruelty beyond what was necessary.

They stopped before a cage larger than the others, positioned in the center of the chamber where it would be visible from every angle. The bars were thick iron, and the lock was complex – clearly designed to hold something strong and potentially dangerous.

"The raptor cage," one guard said, pulling it open. "Prince William had it commissioned years ago, just in case he ever caught one of your kind. Been waiting a long time to use it."

They shoved Kira inside and slammed the door shut. The lock clicked with awful finality. Through the bars, she could see Henry being pushed into a smaller cage nearby, and Elena being chained to a post where she could see everything but do nothing.

As the guards retreated up the stairs, Kira gripped the bars and surveyed her prison. The cage was about ten feet square, tall enough that she could stand upright even if she released her wings. Which she couldn't do... her gown makers had been too efficient.

Around her, in the other cages, creatures stirred. The young centaur. The muzzled dragon. The fairy-like beings. All the specimens in Prince William's collection, now with a new prize addition – a royal raptor to display as proof that even the most hidden could be found and caged.

"Princess?" A small voice came from somewhere in the shadows. "Is that really you?"

Kira's eyes adjusted enough to see a tiny figure pressed against the bars of a nearby cage. One of the flower sprites from that horrible cake, somehow still alive. "You survived," Kira breathed.

"Some of us did," the sprite said. "Hidden in the kitchen when they made the cake. We've been here ever since, hoping..." The tiny voice broke. "We heard you tried to help. That you were working with Elena's network. We had hope, for the first time in so long. And now..."

"Now I've failed you," Kira finished bitterly. "Failed everyone. I'm sorry. I'm so sorry."

"You tried," a deeper voice said from another cage. The young dragon, its scales dull with captivity. "More than anyone else has in years. You stood up to Prince William."

Two tiny voices spoke up from a small cage hidden in the shadows. "You refused to eat what they told you were us!"

Kira practically jumped for joy. *The young trolls!*

"What? How are you alive?"

"Prince William never intended to cook us," one explained, fear still in its voice. "He wanted you to think you'd failed to save us. More torture. He had his cooks prepare some of the turkeys you brought from Latavia, then labeled them with our names. We've been here the whole time, hidden in the back, forced to listen while everyone thought we were dead.

But the other troll had a puzzled voice."Why do you eat turkey? We heard you brought salmon too."

"What good is living without principle?" Elena's voice carried across the chamber, rough but unbroken despite her obvious injuries. "Princess, you want to do the right thing. Not the safe thing, not the strategic thing, but the right thing. And that's worth something, even in failure."

Kira's head dropped. "We didn't think the turkey and salmon were thinking beings," she explained. "I don't know anymore, but was it worth your network being destroyed?" Kira asked. "Worth all those safe houses being raided, those escape routes being sealed? The turkeys dead to save the trolls?"

"The network was already compromised," Elena admitted. "Prince William's been hunting us for months. We knew our time was limited. At least this way, we went down fighting instead of hiding. At least we tried to save some creatures before the end."

"It mattered to us," the trolls said in unison.

Henry's voice came from his cage, strained but steady. "Kira, they are right. We were never going to win here. This castle, this kingdom... it's built on cruelty and maintained by power. The best we could do was refuse to participate, to show that there are people who won't compromise even when threatened. That's not failure. That's witness."

"Witness," Kira repeated numbly. "We're witnesses to horror, trapped in cages, waiting to be executed or worse. That's what my principles bought us."

"No," a new voice said, and Kira's heart nearly stopped. It was small, slightly squeaky, and coming from somewhere near the drainage grate. "Your principles bought us time. And distraction. And an opportunity."

"Freddy?" Kira pressed against the bars, searching for the shadows. "You're still free?"

The frog hopped into the dim torchlight, looking bedraggled but determined. "Free and highly motivated to stay that way. Prince William's guards may have caught Elena's network, but they didn't know about me. And I've spent the last hour exploring these drainage tunnels very, very carefully."

"The tunnels are sealed," Kira said. "Prince William said..."

"Prince William said a lot of things," Freddy interrupted. "Some of them were even true. Yes, the main drainage exits are sealed. But there are older tunnels, smaller ones, that even the Romalanders don't know about. And you know what's really interesting about really old castle construction?"

Despite everything, Kira felt a flicker of something that might have been hope. "What?"

"Old cages have lower locks, almost on the floor," Freddy said. "And lower locks can be opened even by a little frog if you happen to have a set of keys. He hopped closer, and Kira saw the ring of keys clutched in his mouth.

"Guards drop things when they try to cover their ears to stop the noise from a screaming frog!"

"You can't free everyone," Kira said, afraid to let hope fully form. "The castle is full of guards. Prince William knows about the escape plan..."

"I can't free everyone," Freddy agreed. "But I can free some. I can open some of the cages with the smallest creatures, the ones who can fit through the tiny drainage tunnels. And I can get a message to Latavia, warn your father about the coming invasion, tell him what really happened here."

"How?" Henry asked.

"There's a tributary that runs from these tunnels all the way to the river that forms the border,' Freddy explained. I can follow it. Lord Marcus travels with a full delegation – heavy wagons, formal pace. They'll take four days to make that round trip. If I swim day and night without stopping, I can make it in two days, maybe less. That gives me at least a full day's head start to warn your father before Lord Marcus arrives with his lies. And once I reach Latavia, I can tell King Phillip everything. The treaty terms, the breeding chambers, and what happened tonight. All of it."

Kira felt tears stinging her eyes – not from despair now, but from overwhelming gratitude for this small, brave, slightly insane frog who refused to give up even when everything seemed lost.

"Save as many as you can," she said. "The smallest ones, like you said. And yes, get word to my father. Tell him..." She paused, thinking. "Tell him I'm sorry I failed diplomatically, but I'm not sorry I refused to compromise on what matters. Tell him Latavia should fight, should resist, should never become like Romaland, no matter what threats they face."

"I'll tell him," Freddy promised. He began hopping from cage to cage, selecting locks carefully, freeing the tiniest prisoners. Flower sprites fluttered free on gossamer wings. Small woodland creatures scurried toward the drainage grates. A miniature dragon, no larger than a cat, spread wings that had been folded for years and took tentative flight toward freedom. He flew to Henry, who removed the muzzles. The dragon took in a huge breath of air, and a tiny flicker of fire emerged from one of his nostrils.

But it wasn't everyone. The larger creatures, the centaur, the adult dragon, even the young trolls who hadn't been killed for the feast, remained caged. And Kira, Henry, and Elena were still prisoners, still facing whatever punishment Prince William had planned.

But some were saved. That had to count for something.

As the last of the small creatures disappeared into the drainage tunnels and Freddy prepared to follow, he paused at Kira's cage. "For what it's worth, Princess? You're the bravest person I've ever met. Bravest or craziest – probably both. But you made a stand when no one else would. That matters. Even if no one but us ever knows it, it matters."

"Be safe," Kira whispered. "And Freddy? Thank you. For everything."

The frog gave a little bow, solemn and dignified despite his small size. "Thank you for teaching me that principles matter more than survival. Now if you'll excuse me, I have a long swim ahead of me to and a kingdom to save."

He hopped to the drainage grate and disappeared into darkness, his small form the last fragment of hope leaving the chamber.

Kira sank to the floor of her cage, exhausted and emotionally drained. She'd failed to prevent war. Failed to save most of the imprisoned creatures. Failed to protect Elena's network. But she'd also refused to become like Prince William. Refused to compromise her values even when threatened. And she'd helped save some lives, even if it was fewer than she'd hoped.

"Kira," Henry said quietly from his cage. "I'm proud to have stood with you. Whatever comes next."

"Me too," Elena added. "You did the right thing. Never doubt that."

From the remaining caged creatures came soft sounds of agreement. They all said "goodnight" to each other because it was vital that they sleep and be ready for one last stand.

As they drifted off to sleep, they could hear the moon-singer's gentle songs echoing through the castle.

Chapter 9 - Breaking Point

Kira woke to the sound of footsteps: heavy boots, multiple guards, and underneath it all, a deliberate rhythm that suggested someone important was descending the spiral stairs. She pushed herself upright in her cage, wincing at muscles cramped from sleeping on cold stone.

Dawn light filtered through high windows, painting the underground chamber in shades of grey. Around her, the other caged creatures stirred, waking to another day of captivity. The centaur pressed its face against the bars, eyes dull with despair. The adult dragon coiled tighter, as if trying to make itself small enough to disappear.

Prince William emerged from the stairwell, immaculate as always despite the early hour. Behind him came Lord Hawkcroft and a handful of guards, their expressions professionally neutral. But what made Kira's blood run cold was what the guards were dragging between them.

Two massive figures, bound in chains thick enough to restrain horses. Even in chains, even beaten and bloodied, Peek and Aboo were unmistakable.

"No, no, no!" Kira screamed, surging to her feet and gripping the bars. "What did you do? They're citizens of Latavia, protected by diplomatic immunity... "

"You see, when a diplomatic mission fails and war is declared, previous arrangements become void. They are spies. And I've been wanting to add adult conjoined trolls to my collection for years. We separate trolls like this after birth, even if we lose one in the process."

As Romalander soldiers had herded them toward the castle, Peek had realized the truth... they'd been betrayed. The border guards they'd trusted had sent word ahead. The "safe passage" promised had been a trap. In that moment of betrayal, Peek had known it was too late to fight, too late to run. All he could do was stay loyal to each other and hope that somehow, the Princess they'd come to rescue would find a way to escape.

Peek's head lifted at the sound of Kira's voice. One of his eyes was swollen shut, but the other focused on her with desperate recognition. "Princess," he rumbled. "Tried to stop them. We tried."

"They came looking for you," Prince William explained, circling the trolls like a predator assessing prey. "Apparently these simple creatures were worried about their friend. They managed to track you all the way to Romaland – quite impressive. My border guards found them trying to sneak into the castle through the old sewers. Of course, we welcomed them. After all, they're such dear friends of yours."

"Let them go," Kira demanded, her voice shaking with rage. "They've done nothing wrong. They're just worried friends..."

"They're trolls," Prince William interrupted. "Dangerous creatures that somehow convinced Latavia to treat them as equals. But here in Romaland, we understand proper classifications. Trolls are either labor sources or food sources, depending on their size and condition. These two..." He studied Peek and Aboo with the calculating gaze of someone evaluating livestock. "Well, they're certainly large enough to provide several impressive feasts. Though I'm considering keeping them alive for my breeding program. The twin connection is fascinating from a biological perspective."

"You're a monster," Kira spat.

"I'm a realist," Prince William replied, sounding almost bored with the accusation. "And I'm providing you with a lesson, Princess. You tried to save **my** creatures last night, but instead exposed an entire resistance network, compromised Elena's people, all in a futile attempt to free prisoners who were never going to stay free. Now your friends have walked right into my hands because they cared about you. Do you see the pattern? Your compassion doesn't save anyone. It just gives me leverage."

He gestured, and guards began dragging the trolls toward an extra-large cage that had been empty until now. Peek and Aboo struggled weakly, but whatever they'd been through – the capture, the beating, possibly some kind of drug, had left them too weak to effectively resist.

"The question is," Prince William continued, "what are you willing to sacrifice to save them? Will you sign my treaty? Agree to its terms, convince your father to accept Romalander authority over Latavia, in exchange for your friends' lives?"

Kira's mind raced. This was the trap within the trap. Prince William had captured Peek and Aboo specifically to use them against her, to force her to choose between her friends and her kingdom. And the worst part was, she was actually considering it.

"Don't do it, Princess," Aboo called out weakly as guards locked them in the cage. "We knew risks when we came. Better we die free than you sign paper that makes everyone slaves."

"Listen to the creature," Prince William said. "Even trolls understand practical reality better than you seem to. This isn't about your two friends. This is about whether Latavia maintains its dangerous illusions about equality and compassion, or whether it joins the civilized world under proper guidance."

From his own cage, Henry spoke up. "There's a third option. Latavia refuses your terms, prepares for war, and fights to protect its values. You might win eventually, but it won't be the easy conquest you're imagining."

"Perhaps," Prince William acknowledged. "But I have leverage now that I didn't have before. King Phillip's daughter, captured while committing crimes against Romalander sovereignty. His favorite knight who he treated like a son, imprisoned for conspiracy and assault. And his daughter's closest companions... those amusing trolls she's so fond of – scheduled for execution within the week unless she signs my treaty." He smiled. "I'm giving King Phillip a choice: bend or watch everyone he loves die. I wonder which he'll choose?"

"My father won't negotiate with threats," Kira said, though her voice wavered slightly.

"Won't he?" Prince William pulled out a parchment. "I'm sending Lord Marcus back to Latavia this morning with very specific terms. Sign the treaty, accept Romalander authority, and I'll return you, Sir Henry, and your troll friends unharmed. Refuse, and..." He let the implication hang. "Well, I'll at least return bodies. Eventually. After they've served their purpose here."

He handed the parchment to Lord Hawkcroft, who departed up the stairs immediately. Prince William turned back to Kira, his expression almost gentle. "You have until Lord Marcus returns with your father's answer. I estimate two days for travel there, negotiations, and two more to travel back. Use that time wisely, Princess. Reflect on whether your principles are worth the lives of everyone you care about."

"And if my father refuses?" Kira asked.

"Then we proceed with war," Prince William said simply. "I invade Latavia with overwhelming force. Your father's castle falls within weeks. And you get to watch it all from this cage, knowing that your stubbornness led directly to your kingdom's destruction." He moved closer to her cage, his voice dropping. "But there's a simpler path, Princess. Sign the treaty yourself. You're royalty... your signature carries weight. Give me what I want, and I'll release everyone. You can go home with your friends, tell your father you negotiated peace, and Latavia survives under my protection."

"Under your control," Kira corrected.

"Control, protection – the words are interchangeable when you're strong enough to enforce them." Prince William straightened. "Think about it. You have... let's see... four days."

♠

The first day passed in miserable contemplation. Kira sat in her cage, watching Peek and Aboo try to comfort each other despite their own pain and fear.

"We're sorry we came," Peek said quietly during the afternoon. "Made things worse for you."

"You didn't make things worse," Kira replied. "You proved that friendship matters more than safety. That some people, some beings, will risk everything for those they care about. That's not something to apologize for."

"But now Prince William has leverage," Henry pointed out from his cage. He'd been quiet most of the day, clearly working through the strategic implications. "Kira, I hate to say this, but maybe we need to consider his offer. Not the treaty – that's still a trap. But if there's a way to negotiate something smaller, to buy time..."

"There's no negotiating with him," Elena interrupted. Despite her injuries and chains, the cook's voice remained strong. "He'll promise anything to get what he wants, then break every promise once he has it. I've seen him do it dozens of times. The only thing Prince William respects is power, and we don't have any."

"We have truth," Kira said. "We know what he really is. What Romaland really is. And Freddy is carrying that truth back to Latavia right now. My father will know the treaty is a trap. He won't fall for Prince William's manipulations."

"But will he sacrifice you to avoid falling for them?" Elena asked gently. "That's the real question. King Phillip loves you. Can he choose duty over love when the cost becomes personal?"

Kira didn't have an answer to that. She knew what choice she'd want her father to make – refuse the treaty, prepare for war, accept that she'd been captured as a consequence of her own choices. But she also knew what choice a parent might make when facing their child's death.

As night fell on the first day, Kira heard sounds from above – feasting, celebration, music. Prince William was hosting another dinner, probably telling his nobles about the trolls he'd captured, about the Latavian princess caged like a common criminal, about how Romaland's superiority had been proven once again.

The sounds made Kira's blood boil. While she sat helpless in this cage, Prince William was celebrating. Turning her failure into entertainment. Using her captured friends as proof that compassion was weakness.

"Princess?" A small voice came from the darkness near the drainage grate. "Princess, are you there?"

Kira's heart sank. "Freddy? You're supposed to be halfway to Latavia by now!"

The frog hopped into view, looking exhausted and filthy from travel through the drainage system. "I spent most of last night exploring every tunnel and passage beneath this castle. Found where they connect—not just to the river, but upward too. There's an old system, probably older than the castle itself, that leads directly to the main keep. One passage comes out behind a tapestry in Prince William's private study. And that's where I found them; the documents, the maps, everything. A small frog could slip in and out without being seen. Elena could never have managed it.'"

Freddy hopped closer. "I've been exploring all night. His study has everything: military plans, treaties with other kingdoms, and correspondence with spies. And Princess? He's not planning to wait for your father's answer. He's already ordered his armies to mobilize. The invasion starts in five days, whether King Phillip signs the treaty or not."

The revelation hit Kira like a splash of cold water. "The choice he offered my father is meaningless. He's invading either way."

"Exactly," Freddy confirmed. "The treaty was never about peace. It was about getting Latavia to lower its defenses while he prepared to attack. If your father signs, Prince William gets control without a fight. If he refuses, Prince William uses that as justification for an invasion he was planning anyway."

Henry let out a string of curses creative enough to make even the dragon look impressed. "So, we're out of options. War is coming no matter what we do."

"Not necessarily," Kira said slowly, an idea forming. "Freddy, you said you can get into Prince William's study through the old passages?"

"Yes, but..."

"And his military plans are there? Battle strategies, troop movements, supply lines?"

"All of it," Freddy confirmed. "He's been planning this invasion for months. Everything is documented."

Kira turned to Henry. "If we could get that information to my father before the invasion starts, he could prepare. Position troops, reinforce borders, maybe even strike first at vulnerable supply depots."

"That's assuming we could get the information out of this castle," Henry pointed out. "We're locked in cages, Freddy is one small frog, and Prince William has guards everywhere."

"We need a distraction," Kira said, her mind racing. "Something big enough to pull guards away from the breeding chambers. Something that would make Prince William focus on protecting his castle instead of watching prisoners."

Elena's eyes widened with understanding. "You're thinking about freeing all the rest of the creatures. Creating enough chaos that in the confusion, someone could reach Prince William's study and steal those military plans."

"It's suicide," Henry said flatly.

"Probably," Kira agreed. "But what's the alternative? Sit here for three more days, wait for Lord Marcus to return, watch my father make an impossible choice based on false options? Or let Prince William invade Latavia unprepared?" She looked at each of her companions. "I'd rather die trying to do something useful than live knowing I could have helped and chose safety instead."

"I'm in," Elena said immediately. "My network is already destroyed. Might as well make my last act count for something."

"We in too," Peek rumbled.

Despite everything, Kira almost smiled. "Aboo?"

The other troll nodded. "We came to help Princess. I still want to help, even if helping means dying. Better than cage."

"Henry?" Kira looked at her best friend, knowing he'd follow her into anything, but wanting him to choose freely anyway.

Henry met her eyes, and she saw resignation, fear, determination, and something that looked like pride all mixed together. "You're completely insane. You know that, right?"

"I've been told," Kira acknowledged.

"And this plan has almost no chance of success."

"Also been told."

"And we'll probably all die in the attempt."

"Starting to see a pattern here," Kira said dryly.

He was making his own choice now—not following automatically but deciding consciously that standing with her mattered more than survival. "I could tell you to stay safe and help with the escape. But that's not who we are, is it?"

He looked at her face and didn't need an answer. Henry sighed. "Then I'm in. Because apparently I'm completely insane too, and because someone needs to watch your back while you're being heroically stupid."

Freddy was quiet for a moment; his large eyes fixed on the drainage grate. He could leave now, swim downriver, and save himself. He'd already done more than any small frog should be able to accomplish. But leaving meant abandoning the creatures still in cages, meant accepting that evil would continue unopposed. He thought of his own years hiding in the shadows of Castle Latavia, always running, always afraid. For once, he chose to fight instead. He was "all in."

Freddy hopped up and down with what might have been excitement or terror – hard to tell with frogs. "So, we're really doing this? Breaking everyone out, stealing military intelligence, and escaping from the most heavily guarded castle in Romaland?"

"That's the plan," Kira confirmed.

"Just checking," Freddy said. "Because it sounds completely impossible when you say it out loud like that."

"Most of our best plans do," Kira replied. She turned her attention to the practical details. "Freddy, you'll need bring as many creatures as you can back here and the keys.

"Already know where most are hiding," Freddy confirmed. "I'll have them here within an hour."

"Good. Once they are here, they can stand on each other's shoulders and open the lock to Henry's. One he's out of his cage, he needs to free the others quietly. No alarms until we're ready." Kira looked around the chamber, counting the caged creatures. "Peek, Aboo, you're the strongest. You'll break the drainage grate bars to make an exit large enough for everyone. It'll be loud, so that has to happen right before we run."

"We can break bars," Peek confirmed. "Trolls very strong when properly motivated. We can also get that muzzle off of the big dragon."

"The centaur is fastest," Kira continued, looking at the young creature in its cage. "You'll follow Freddy to Prince William's study, gather the documents, then get him and satchel to the drainage tunnels. Can you do that?"

The centaur nodded, speaking for the first time since Kira's capture. "I can run. Been waiting for years for a chance to run free. I won't fail you."

"The dragon can provide air cover once we're outside," Kira said. "Breathe fire, create smoke, distract guards while others escape."

The dragon lifted its head, scales brightening slightly. "Haven't flown in three years. Might be clumsy. But I'll give them something to remember and have that little guy help me."

"Elena, you know this castle better than anyone. You'll guide the smaller creatures to the drainage tunnels. Get as many out as possible before the guards respond. No more hiding, time fight."

"And you?" Elena asked. "What will you be doing?"

Kira's expression hardened. "I'm going to find Prince William. While everyone else is escaping, while he's dealing with chaos and confusion, I'm going to have a conversation with him about the cost of treating thinking beings as property."

"That's not a conversation," Henry said. "That's a suicide mission."

"Maybe," Kira acknowledged. "But he needs to understand that Latavia won't be conquered easily. Even caged and outnumbered, we'll fight back. Sometimes the most important thing isn't winning – it's making sure they know they were in a fight."

♠

Freddy returned within an hour with the keys, soaking wet from his journey through the drainage system but triumphant. He was followed by the little dragon and the young trolls. "Got them.

Got help. The lock on Henry's wooden door is four feet high and these three on my shoulders – are exactly four feet! Also, I checked on the passages while I was moving around. The route to the river is clear, but guards have been posted near some of the drainage exits. We'll need to be fast once the alarm is raised."

"How long do you think we have?" Kira asked as Freddy and his team stood on each other and unlocked Henry's door.

"From the moment we break out until guards arrive in force? Maybe five minutes if we're lucky. Ten if the dragon creates enough chaos topside. After that, we'll be fighting running battles through the castle." Freddy's large eyes were serious. "Princess, a lot of us aren't going to make it. The slower creatures, the injured ones, anyone who gets caught in the initial confusion – they'll be recaptured or killed."

"I know," Kira said quietly. "But staying in these cages guarantees they'll never be free. At least this way, some have a chance."

Henry began unlocking cages, moving as quietly as possible. Each creature he freed received whispered instructions – stay quiet, wait for the signal, then run for the drainage tunnels. Don't stop, don't look back, just run.

The moon-singer stretched her wings that hadn't been spread in years. The forest sprites hovered uncertainly, unused to freedom. The small dragon tested its limbs, preparing for flight it hadn't attempted since its capture. One by one, the cages emptied until only the largest remained.

Henry unlocked Kira's cage, and she emerged stiffly, rubbing her shoulders where the cage's low ceiling had forced her to crouch. Then she grabbed the keys and moved to Peek and Aboo's cage, the keys clicking in the lock with a sound that seemed impossibly loud in the tense silence.

The twin trolls shuffled out, testing their chains. The bonds were thick iron, locked with mechanisms Kira couldn't open. But Peek just grinned; a terrifying expression on a troll's face, and flexed his massive arms. The chains groaned, stretched, and finally snapped with a sound like breaking thunder.

"Guess we're done being quiet now," Aboo observed. He immediately moved to the dragon's cage.

"Hold still, friend. These muzzles got a weak point." With surprisingly gentle fingers for such massive hands, the trolls worked at the leather and metal constraining the dragon's snout, finding the stressed joint where constant pressure had weakened the mechanism. With a sharp twist, the muzzle cracked and fell away. The dragon took its first full breath in years, small wisps of smoke already curling from its nostrils.

Aboo spotted the young trolls and screamed as he picked them both up. "Can I keep them, Princess?"

Above them, shouts erupted. Guards responding to the noise, probably calling for reinforcements. The alarm bells began ringing, deep, resonant clangs that echoed through the castle.

"Now!" Kira shouted. "Drainage grate, break it now!"

Peek and Aboo charged the metal grate covering the largest drainage tunnel, hitting it in perfect synchronization. The old iron shrieked but held. They backed up and hit it again, harder this time, and the grate tore free from its moorings with a sound of protesting metal.

"Go, go, go!" Elena was already herding the smaller creatures toward the opening, pushing them into the darkness of the tunnel beyond. The centaur galloped forward, and Freddy leaped onto its back, clinging to its mane as it plunged into the drainage system.

Guards began pouring down the stairs, swords drawn. The dragon surged past Kira, muzzle torn free by Peek and Aboo earlier, wings finally spreading fully, and launched itself at the guards with a roar that shook the chamber. Fire bloomed in the stairwell, and men screamed, falling back.

"The dragon's buying us time!" Henry shouted over the chaos. "But we need to move!"

"You move!" Kira shouted back. "Get everyone out! I have something I need to do!"

Before Henry could argue, Kira was running – not toward the drainage tunnels and escape, but toward the stairs and deeper into the castle. She could hear Henry cursing behind her, ordering

Peek and Aboo to get the creatures to safety while he followed her into madness.

Because that's what friends did, they followed you into madness and tried to keep you alive while you were being stupidly heroic, Kira thought.

Kira burst through the stairwell where the dragon had scattered the guards, using their moment of confusion to slip past. Behind her, she heard Henry's footsteps and knew he'd followed despite her orders. Part of her was grateful. Another part was furious that he'd put himself in more danger.

Most of her was too focused on what came next to care about either emotion.

She was going to find Prince William. And she was going to show him that even caged princesses had claws.

Chapter 10 - A New Kind of Treaty

The castle had descended into chaos. Alarm bells rang from every tower, guards ran in all directions shouting contradictory orders, and somewhere in the distance, the dragon was creating magnificent havoc – its roars echoing through stone corridors, fire blooming in the night sky visible through windows Kira passed.

She ran through corridors she'd walked as a diplomatic guest just days ago, but now everything looked different. The elegant tapestries were just hiding places for secrets. The polished floors were surfaces to slip on while fighting. The grand architecture was a maze designed to confuse and trap.

Henry caught up to her at a junction where three hallways met. "What's the plan?" he gasped, sword drawn and ready.

"Find Prince William," Kira said. "Make him understand what it costs to cage thinking beings."

"And then what? Fight him? Kill him? Start a war we're already losing?"

"I don't know!" Kira admitted, her voice cracking with frustration and fear and fury all mixed together. "I just know I can't leave without facing him. Without making him see me – really see me – not as a prize to be collected or an enemy to be caged, but as someone who fought back. Someone who refused to be broken."

Henry grabbed her arm, stopping her. "Kira. Listen to yourself. You're talking about suicide for the sake of symbolic gesture. That's not brave, it's wasteful. Your kingdom needs you alive, not dead in Prince William's castle making a point he won't even understand."

"My kingdom needs someone who won't compromise with monsters!" Kira shot back. "Someone who'll stand up and say 'no more' even when it's hopeless. Because if I don't, if I just run away, then Prince William wins. He breaks me without even having to kill me."

"He already won," Henry said brutally. "He captured us, destroyed Elena's network, and provoked the war he wanted. Nothing you do now changes that."

"But it changes me," Kira insisted. "Don't you see? Every time I've compromised, every time I've swallowed my rage and played diplomatic games, a piece of me died. I ate that cursed cake. I saw horrors and smiled. I can't leave here having never stood up to him directly. Having never shown him that Latavian values are worth dying for."

Henry stared at her for a long moment. Then, slowly, his expression shifted from frustration to understanding to grim determination. "All right. Then we do this together. We find Prince William, we deliver whatever message you need to deliver, and then we get out alive if possible. Deal?"

"Deal," Kira agreed, relief flooding through her. She wasn't alone in this madness. She'd never been alone.

They moved deeper into the castle, following the sounds of organized response. Prince William would be wherever the commanders were gathering, wherever orders were being coordinated. And sure enough, as they climbed to the upper levels, they heard his voice cutting through the chaos.

"I don't care how many you have to kill, I want every escaped creature hunted down and returned to its cage! And find the princess! She's more valuable alive but I'll settle for her corpse if necessary!"

Kira and Henry exchanged glances. Then, together, they stepped around the corner into Prince William's war room.

The chamber was full of nobles and commanders, all clustered around a large table covered with maps and tactical documents. Prince William stood at the head, still dressed in his evening finery, looking more annoyed than concerned by the chaos his prisoners had created.

Every eye turned as Kira walked in, blood-spattered and defiant, with Henry at her back.

"Looking for me?" Kira asked.

For just a moment, genuine surprise crossed Prince William's face. Then his expression smoothed into cold fury. "Guards! Seize them!"

"Before you do," Kira said loudly, her voice carrying across the room, "you should know that while your guards were chasing escaped prisoners, one of them reached your private study. All your military plans, the invasion timetables, troop movements, supply routes, they're gone. Being carried to Latavia as we speak by creatures you considered too insignificant to guard against. They will be there before Lord Marcus arrives."

The color drained from Prince William's face. "You're lying."

"Am I?" Kira smiled without humor. "Send someone to check. See if your precious documents are still behind that tapestry in your study."

Prince William gestured sharply, and two guards ran from the room. The remaining nobles were muttering among themselves, clearly alarmed by the implications. If Latavia had their invasion plans, the element of surprise was gone. The careful strategies Prince William had been developing for months were worthless.

"Even if you've stolen my plans," Prince William said, his voice tight with controlled rage, "it changes nothing. Romaland still has overwhelming force. Latavia will still fall."

"Maybe," Kira acknowledged. "But now we'll be ready. We'll meet your armies at our borders instead of in our heartland. We'll fortify your expected attack routes and ambush your supply lines. We'll make you fight for every inch of ground, and we'll make sure the whole world knows why... because Romaland treats thinking beings as livestock. We'll meet with South Romaland and tell them about your cages and your 'united civilization' is built on systematic cruelty. You cage and kill creatures for having the audacity to be intelligent while not being human. The south will never join up with you."

"I'm going to make sure every kingdom, every ruler, every person who might consider allying with you knows exactly what Romaland is. What you are. And then they can decide if your strength is worth the cost of their conscience."

The guards returned, their faces confirming what Kira already knew. The documents were gone. Prince William's carefully laid plans were in enemy hands.

"You've just guaranteed your own death," Prince William said softly, dangerously. "And Henry's. And every creature that escaped tonight. I'll hunt them all down, and I'll make examples of them. And when South Romaland hears what you did—how you hunted intelligent beings for sport—they'll distance themselves from us, not support our unification. You've given them exactly the excuse they needed to stay independent and claim the moral high ground.'"

"You'll try," Kira corrected. "But hunting is harder when your prey knows you're coming. When they're prepared, armed, and fighting for survival. Both the adult and little dragon are breathing fire again." She took a step forward. "I came here as a diplomat, trying to prevent war. But you never wanted peace. You wanted submission dressed up as alliance. So now you have war. And Latavia will fight with everything we have."

"A war you can't win," Prince William reminded her.

"Probably not," Kira admitted. "But we'll fight anyway. Because some things are worth fighting for even when you know you'll lose. Dignity. Freedom. The right to choose compassion over cruelty." She met his eyes directly. "And the absolute certainty that your way is wrong, no matter how many armies enforce it."

The room had gone silent. Even the nobles who'd been muttering had stopped to watch this confrontation between a blood-spattered princess and the prince who'd thought he'd broken her.

"You know what the funny thing is?" Kira continued. "You thought catching me would give you leverage over my father. You thought I'd be a prize to display or a hostage to manipulate. But you were wrong. Because my mother taught me that a wiser ruler's first duty is to their people, not their family. If I die here tonight, he'll mourn me. But he won't surrender to save me. That's what Latavian values really mean; loving people enough to let them die for what matters."

"How touching," Prince William said coldly. "Guards!" But before the guards could move, another voice cut through the chaos. It was an older, stronger voice.

"Wait." The voice came from Lord Hawkcroft, the military commander. He stepped forward, his face thoughtful. "Prince William, if Latavia has our invasion plans, we need to reconsider our timing. Possibly our entire approach. A prepared enemy is vastly more difficult to conquer than a surprised one. Our casualties would be tripled. The Northern nobles trust my tactical judgment. If we proceed and lose soldiers unnecessarily, the political repercussions could be severe."

"Are you questioning my authority?" But Prince William's voice quickly dropped to a whisper when he saw the serious look on his father's closest friend's face.

"I'm doing my job as military commander," Lord Hawkcroft replied steadily. "Which is to ensure Romaland wins its wars with minimal losses. If we proceed with the invasion while Latavia knows our every move, we'll still probably win, but at a cost that might not be worthwhile. I took the liberty of writing up a new treaty with Latavia using your original but removing the items that were... hard to swallow." He winked at Kira and Henry.

"Your father has signed it. We only need the council to approve it."

Other nobles began nodding, murmuring agreement. Kira could see the logic in their eyes. Maintaining Prince William's pride was not worth the blood and gold it would cost them. What if King Stephen lived for a few more years?

Prince William saw it too. His expression darkened as he realized his nobles were wavering, that Kira's defiance had introduced doubt into what should have been a simple conquest.

"Get out," he said finally, his voice flat. "Princess Kira, Sir Henry, get out of my castle and out of my kingdom."

Tell your father that the only reason I'm letting you leave is because killing you now would make you a martyr. I'd rather you live to see Latavia fall."

Kira wanted to argue, to press her advantage, to do something more than just leave. But Henry's hand on her arm steadied her, reminded her that they'd accomplished what they came for, a new treaty that Lord Hawkcroft was holding out for them to take. Plus, they'd stolen the invasion plans and bought Latavia time to prepare.

"One more thing," Kira said as they turned to leave. "The creatures that escaped tonight? The ones from your breeding chambers? They're not your property to hunt down. They're free beings making their own choices. And if your soldiers pursue them into Latavian territory, we'll consider it an act of war. A war that you started."

"The war was always coming. I just made sure we'd fight it on our terms instead of yours."

As they left the war room, Kira took the treaty from Lord Hawkcroft. As they made their way through the still-chaotic castle toward the stables, Henry let out a shaky breath. "I can't believe that worked."

"Worked is a strong word," Kira replied. "We're still in enemy territory, we've been given until dawn to leave, and we've just guaranteed that war is coming."

"But we're alive," Henry pointed out. "And we got the invasion plans and I no longer wonder about my Romalander roots. You faced Prince William down without backing down. That's more than I expected when you went running off to find him."

They reached the stables to find their horses and as Kira mounted Julius, she heard a familiar voice call out: "Princess! Wait!"

The centaur galloped forward, the leather satchel containing Prince William's stolen documents still secured across its back; the military plans that had been too large and numerous for Freddy to carry alone, requiring the centaur's strength and speed to escape the castle.

Elena emerged from the shadows, supported by two other escapees. She looked awful, bruised and bleeding, but alive.

"I thought you were getting everyone out through the drainage tunnels and moving towards South Romaland," Kira said.

"I got most of them out," Elena confirmed. "The rest..." She shook her head. "We did what we could. But I couldn't leave without thanking you. For trying. For caring. For refusing to be broken."

"I didn't save you," Kira pointed out. "You're injured, your network is destroyed, and you're about to be hunted by every soldier in North Romaland."

"But I'm free," Elena replied simply. "For the first time in years, I made a choice that mattered. I helped beings escape instead of watching them suffer. That's worth whatever comes next." She pressed something into Kira's hand – a small gold feather pendant, matching the one Prince William had torn from her neck. "For when you need to remember that resistance matters, even when it seems hopeless."

Kira closed her fingers around the pendant, feeling its weight. "Come with us. You and the others. Latavia will give you sanctuary, if South Romaland won't."

"I will," Elena said. "But not yet. Some of Prince William's nobles are wavering. The doubt you created, the questions you raised about whether this type of society is worth fighting for. Those nobles need encouragement. Need someone to whisper in their ears about the cost of conquest, about what happened to the last kingdoms that allied with Romaland, about whether Prince William's vision regarding creature breeding is worth following to its inevitable end."

"You're staying to work against him from inside," Kira realized.

"I'm staying to plant seeds of doubt," Elena corrected. "Resistance doesn't always look like escape or rebellion. Sometimes it looks like quiet voices asking uncomfortable questions. You did the dramatic part – the escape, the defiance, the grand confrontation. Now let me do the boring part – the slow work of eroding confidence in a system built on cruelty."

"Be careful," Kira said. "Please. Prince William won't be kind if he discovers what you're doing."

"Probably not," Elena agreed. "But I spent years being careful and watching creatures die. I'm done being careful."

She stepped back, and the centaur moved forward. On its back, clinging tightly, was Freddy, who pointed up to the sky.

"The invasion plans," Freddy announced proudly. "Every document we got out; troop numbers, supply routes, timelines, everything."

"The dragons!" Henry exclaimed. "I see the satchel on the big one's back."

"You're a miracle," Kira breathed. "Freddy, you saved Latavia tonight."

"We saved Latavia," Freddy corrected. "You created the chaos that let me work. Elena's network showed me the passages. The centaur got me in and out. I convinced the dragons not to eat me. And now we all get to run very fast before Prince William changes his mind about letting you leave alive." He hopped from the centaur onto Julius's saddle behind Kira. "So how about we stop celebrating and start riding?"

The centaur spoke up, its young voice stronger now that it had tasted freedom. "I'll come too. To Latavia. I can help carry messages, scout ahead, fight if needed. I owe you that much."

"You owe us nothing," Kira said. "But you're welcome in Latavia. All creatures who value freedom are."

"Speaking of freedom," a deep voice rumbled from the darkness. Peek and Aboo emerged, with the young trolls on their shoulders. Several smaller creatures clustered around them – forest sprites, the small dragon, and others who'd escaped the breeding chambers. "We stick with Princess. Make sure she gets home safe."

Kira looked at the small group assembled around her; escaped prisoners, resistance members, creatures who should have been caged or killed but had chosen defiance instead. They weren't an army. They weren't even particularly well-armed. But they were free, and they were fighting for something that mattered.

"All right," she said. "We ride for the border. Stay together, help anyone who falls behind, and don't stop for anything. Latavia's two days away at a hard pace.

With the dragons circling overhead, breathing fire at soldiers who tried to shoot it down, smoke rose from several buildings where the chaos had spread. And somewhere in that castle, Prince William was realizing that his perfect trap had fallen apart, but he smiled when he read a copy of the new treaty.

♠

By the time they crossed into Latavian territory on the morning of the second day, they were battered, bleeding, and running on nothing but determination and fear. But they were alive. And they had the intelligence that might save their kingdom.

Latavian border guards and knights spotted them and rushed forward with weapons drawn, then gasped in recognition. "Princess Kira! We thought... our spies sent word that Prince William had executed you!"

"He wishes," Kira replied, sliding off Julius on legs that barely held her. "Get word to my father immediately. Tell him I'm alive and that I'm bringing critical intelligence about Romaland's invasion plans. War is coming." She pulled out the new treaty and handed it to one of the knights. "Take this to my father."

As the knight rode off, Kira finally allowed herself to sink to the ground, Henry collapsing beside her. Around them, their companions did the same – creatures and humans alike, all pushed past their limits, all having survived what should have been impossible.

"We did it," Henry said wonderingly. "We actually did it."

"We started it," Kira corrected. "The hard part comes next, preparing our people for invasion. Making sure the intelligence we stole actually helps instead of just delaying the inevitable."

"Always looking on the bright side," Freddy muttered from where he'd sprawled on a rock, too exhausted even to hop.

"Someone has to be realistic," Kira replied. But despite her words, she felt something she hadn't felt since entering Prince William's castle... hope. Not hope that everything would be fine, or that Latavia would defeat Romaland's armies. But if they could keep North and South Romaland from joining forces. She knew the people from the south were vegan. Maybe if she could get Latavians to give up their chicken, turkeys, and fish...

♠

King Phillip was waiting when they reached the castle. He stood at the gates with Queen Selina, his face a mixture of relief and fear and fury all tangled together.

The moment Kira dismounted, he pulled her into a crushing embrace. "You foolish, brave, impossible child," he whispered. "When word came that you'd been captured, that Prince William was demanding our surrender as ransom..."

"You didn't consider it, did you?" Kira pulled back to look at him. "Tell me you didn't."

"Of course I considered it," King Phillip replied. "You're my daughter. I'd burn the world to keep you safe." He cupped her face gently. "But you're also my heir. And you needed me to be a king, not just a father. So, I prepared for war instead of surrender. And prayed to all the ancient laws that you'd find a way to survive."

"I did more than survive," Kira said. She gestured to the dragons, who landed and dropped the leather satchel at her feet. "We stole Prince William's invasion plans. Troop movements, supply routes, timeline, allied kingdoms – everything he was hiding. And we brought proof of what Romaland really is. What they do to thinking beings who aren't human or who have traits they consider 'unnatural.'"

King Phillip took the satchel, his expression hardening as he understood the implications. "Then we have a chance. Not a guarantee, but a chance." He looked at the assembled group; the escaped creatures, the exhausted companions, the evidence of everything they'd endured. "Everyone inside. You'll tell me everything while healers tend your injuries. And then we'll plan how Latavia will face what's coming."

"Did you read the new treaty?" Kira asked her father.

He nodded. "There is a term that I don't understand, but my council is studying it and writing a new treaty based on the information you provided us. We'll talk about it later."

"Princess?" The small dragon landed on her shoulder, its scales warm against her neck. "What happens now?"

"Now?" Kira considered the question. "Now we prepare for war. We fortify our borders, train our soldiers, and make alliances with other kingdoms who might be willing to stand against Romaland's expansion. We take the intelligence we stole and use it to turn Prince William's careful plans into chaos. He'll probably sign our new treaty to buy himself more time to get south on his side."

"And we keep rescuing creatures," Peek added, lumbering up beside her. "From Romaland, from anywhere. Show everyone that Latavia stands for something different. Something better."

"A sanctuary," Henry said thoughtfully. "Not just a kingdom, but a place where being different or having non-human heritage doesn't make you property. Where thinking beings are judged by their choices, not their species."

King Phillip, overhearing, nodded slowly. "A dangerous vision. One that Prince William and others like him will fight to destroy."

"Then we'll defend it," Kira said simply. "Not because we're guaranteed to win, but because it's worth defending. Because the alternative, becoming like Romaland, adopting their classifications and cruelties, would be a worse defeat than any military loss."

Her father studied her for a long moment, and Kira saw something shift in his expression. Pride, yes, but also recognition. She'd left as a princess, trying to play diplomatic games. She'd returned as a leader who understood the cost of principles and chose them anyway.

"You're right," King Phillip said finally. "And you'll help me build this sanctuary, this new Latavia that stands openly for what we've always believed privately. It won't be easy. We'll be challenged, threatened, and possibly invaded. But we'll face it together."

That evening, Latavia held a council of war. But it wasn't just military commanders and nobles who attended. Kira had insisted on including the escaped creatures, Elena's resistance members who'd made it to Latavia, and representatives from the enchanted forest who'd heard about the coming conflict. Kira had brought in a few turkeys but they didn't seem to understand why they were there.

As maps were spread and plans were made, as alliances were proposed and strategies debated, Kira looked around the room and saw what Romaland would never understand. Strength came not from dominating the weak, but from empowering them. Not from enforcing hierarchies, but from choosing cooperation. Not from treating others as resources, but from recognizing them as allies.

Prince William had five armies, sophisticated weapons, and an overwhelming force.

But Latavia had something he could never build with all his power, a coalition of beings who chose to stand together because they believed in something worth protecting. Not land or resources or power, but the simple, radical idea that all thinking beings deserve dignity, freedom, and the right to choose their own paths.

It might not be enough to win the war. But it was worth fighting for. And in fighting for it, they would forge a new kind of treaty, not between kingdoms, but between all beings who valued compassion over conquest. The conversion to being vegans would create a lot of resistance, especially from Peek and Aboo, but Kira was determined to never eat another species again.

♠

Epilogue

Prince William stood at the crest of Widow's Hill, his army assembled behind him like a dark tide waiting to break. The morning sun caught on polished armor and sharpened steel, transforming his forces into a field of deadly mirrors. But his smile held no warmth as he surveyed the Latavian encampment below.

"Your Highness," Owen approached, still uncomfortable in the black armor that had replaced his usual simple garb. The weight of his new title, Knight of War, that replaced his old title of Knight of Defense, sat heavier on his shoulders than his armor. "The men await your command."

"Patience, Sir Owen." William's voice carried the satisfaction of a cat cornering a mouse. "Let them wonder. Let them worry. This is all part of the exercise."

"Exercise, Your Highness?"

"War Games." William savored the words like fine wine. "A small clause I put in the new treaty that King Phillip insisted we sign. Two kingdoms practice the art of war without the inconvenience of actual death. Think of it... all the strategy, all the glory, none of the tedious burial duties."

Owen's stomach churned. He wanted to prevent bloodshed, not to orchestrate elaborate charades of it. "And the Latavians agreed to this?"

"They signed the new treaty." William's determination was absolute. "When five armies appear at your border, calling it a game, what choice do you have but to play along? Besides, Princess Kira is clever and a fighter. She'll understand the opportunity this presents."

"Opportunity?"

"To test ourselves. To push boundaries. To discover what we're truly capable of when the stakes are..." William paused, his eyes gleaming with private knowledge, "theoretical."

A horn sounded from the Latavian camp—not an alarm, but a question rendered in brass and wind. They'd been seen.

"Send the herald," William commanded. "Inform Princess Kira that the Kingdom of Romaland invites Latavia to participate in the first official War Games as outlined in the new treaty. Seven days of mock combat. Controlled engagements. Points for objectives. All very civilized."

Owen bowed, though his heart rebelled. As he turned to relay the orders, William's voice stopped him.

"Oh, and Owen? Do mention that refusing to participate would be... a violation of the new treaty? And we wouldn't want anyone to think the Latavians are afraid of a simple game, would we? Make sure you tell that to the princess."

An Excerpt from Book 4 – War Games

Kira's wings ached where the silk-snake's threads had bitten deep. Even now, freed from their burning touch, she could feel the poison of them in her bones, inhibiting her ability to transform. The cave stank of damp stone and betrayal.

"You're awake." Charles's voice came from the shadows, still wearing that concerned mask he'd perfected over years of friendship. "I was worried the chains might have...

"Don't." Kira's voice cracked like a whip. "Don't you dare pretend to care."

He stepped into the flickering torchlight, and for a moment, she saw genuine pain flicker across his features. Charles, who had trained beside her since childhood. Charles, who had covered for her when she'd first started experiencing transformations. Charles, who had sworn on his mother's grave to keep her secret.

"You don't understand," he said quietly. "What you're becoming... it changes everything. The old bloodlines, the traditional power structures, they'll all become obsolete. Do you have any idea what that means?"

"Evolution," Kira spat. "Progress. A chance for our people to become something greater."

"Chaos." Charles's calm certainty was more frightening than anger would have been. "The strong will soar while the weak are left behind. Families that have ruled for generations will be overthrown by anyone lucky enough to manifest powers. It will tear both kingdoms apart."

"So, you decided to start a war instead?"

He moved closer, just out of reach. "The blood moon rises tonight, Kira. If we can maintain the old ways through these seven days, if we can prove that steel and strategy matter more than wings and magic, then maybe..."

The sound of her laughter cut him off. It wasn't bitter or angry. It was genuinely amusing.

"You think you can stop evolution with a sword?" She flexed her shoulders, feeling the first stirrings of transformation returning despite the silk-snakes' lingering effects. "You think you can hold back the tide with tradition?"

"I think," Charles said, backing toward the cave entrance, "that you're about to do something reckless."

Kira's grin was all predator. "You have no idea."

The chains had weakened her, yes. But they hadn't broken her. And Charles had made one crucial error in his calculations—he'd assumed she needed her full strength to escape.

He'd never considered what she might become when cornered.

The transformation that rippled through her wasn't the graceful unfurling of wings she'd grown accustomed to. It was raw, primal, powered by necessity and fury. When it ended, she stood before him as something entirely new, neither fully human nor completely other.

"Run," she told him, and her gravel-like voice carried a deep rumble that made the cave walls tremble.

Charles ran.

And somewhere in the distance, the blood moon began its rise.

The Complete Kira and Henry Series:

- Book 1: Quest into the Forbidden Lands
- Book 2: Lost in the Enchanted Forest
- Book 3: Dangerous Treaty
- Book 4: War Games (Coming Soon)
- Book 5: Edict of Love (Coming Soon)
- Book 6: King Kira (Coming Soon)

About the Author

Sandi Jerome is a writer and graduate of UCLA's Advanced Screenwriting program. Her screenplay, *Runaway Cricket*, is being produced as an animated musical by BlackOrb.com. She has been a finalist in most of the major contests, Nicholls, Page International and Austin Film Festival.

Sandi grew up on an avocado farm in Escondido and was the "go to" kid to climb up high and pick the top fruit. She would then jump down into the thick pile of leaves and thought she could fly! She created this young adult fantasy series, *Kira and Henry*, where the teen princess must hide the secret that she can fly or be banished from the kingdom. The first book, Kira and Henry: *Quest into the Forbidden Lands*, was a 2nd Rounder in 2023 Austin Film Festival and a 2024 Kindle Book Review finalist.

Sandi is an enrolled and blood member of the Cherokee Nation and a two-time winner of the Native American Media Alliance fellowship. In her first NAMA TV writing fellowship, she wrote *Technically Soccer*, a half-hour comedy about a Women's Professional Soccer team getting an AI-Robot coach. Sandi is an avid women's soccer fan; she coached and played soccer for over twenty years. *Blood Moon Wolf* (TV Pilot and Feature) was completed as part of her 2nd Native American fellowship, about a wolf who turns into a girl to become a spirit guide. Her middle-grade book, *Sleep Warrior*, about her Cherokee ancestor, was #3 on Coverfly's Red List of Animated Manuscripts. To get her message into schools, she is seeking a more traditional publisher for her Native American books.

As a Floridian and a long-time Disney fan, annual passholder, and certified Disney expert, Sandi wrote *Pixie Dust Death* set at Disney World, then created a non-Disney version, *Wilma Wallaby Genius Girl Detective,* set at a theme park she invented, and the series bible to be developed into a kids' series by a UK

Production company. She is also the author of the *Amazing Animals of Disney's Animal Kingdom.*

Sandi wrote a book adaptation of *Hijacked* for producer Melissa Shevela of Helicopter Productions. Her next book adaptation to film was Jake and Clara based on the book, *Jake & Clara: Scandal, Politics, Hollywood and Murder* by Wall Street Journal bestselling author, ghostwriter, broadcaster, David R. Stokes. Blair Underwood optioned David's previous book. She and David wrote a book very personal to Sandi, *Churchill's Mum: The Story of Jennie Jerome,* after years of research connecting Sandi's husband, Keith, to the American heiress who was Winston Churchill's mother and Keith's fifth cousin. It presents the premise that Winston's half-American status helped defeat Hitler. She had done almost a dozen "writer for hire" gigs that involved book adaptations or co-writing books with producers who had a great idea.

Sandi is a scientist and loves designing edible gardens and doing botany experiments. Her early fascination with science and the nearby San Onofre Nuclear Generating Station inspired her to write an action script, *Use of Deadly Force*. Her husband was a technical writer in the nuclear industry and ensured the authenticity of her work. She belonged to a Science and Technology group and helped develop a volunteer Web on Wheels program that brought email to residents of assisted living centers. This inspired her body-switching comedy, *Time for Lily*, which was a First-Round Finalist in Script Magazine Open Door Contest. She is working on a technical book on salt-tolerant plants with her biologist granddaughter.

She wrote a Sci-Fi thriller script, *Last Woman*, that explores the multiverse and technology gone awry. It was a semifinalist in Final Draft's Big Break contest. Sandi was the first editor of *Digital Dealer* Magazine and wrote computer software reviews for major publications and numerous published computer guides. She sold her technology company in 2022, and now writes full-time, at least 10 pages a day.

For Sandi, "Writing is life!"

Learn more at www.**SandraJerome**.com or leave comments on her publisher's Contact page, www.**SmilingEagle**.com.

www.ingramcontent.com/pod-product-compliance
Lightning Source LLC
Chambersburg PA
CBHW071158300726

48975CB00004B/1198